SEAL ON THE SHORE

'Keep still!' Mandy gasped with the effort of freeing the trapped animal and carrying it struggling to the water. 'Hold on; I'm coming in!' She took a wide step from rock to boat, holding the seal pup in her arms.

The boat lurched and rocked sideways. Mandy kept her balance, feeling the waves splash in round her ankles. She gave a little cry.

'It's OK, you made it. Put her in the bottom here.' Ross watched Mandy lay the sick pup in the pool of salt water at their feet. Then he picked up the oars and rowed.

'Quick, Ross. Let's get her home as fast as we can!'

LUCY DANIELS

Seal
— *on the* —
Shore

Illustrated by Jenny Gregory

**Hodder
Children's
Books**

a division of Hodder Headline plc

Special thanks to Jenny Oldfield
Thanks also to C. J. Hall, B.Vet.Med., M.R.C.V.S., for reviewing
the veterinary information contained in this book.

Text copyright © 1997 Ben M. Baglio
Created by Ben M. Baglio, London W6 0HE
Illustrations copyright © 1997 Jenny Gregory

First published in Great Britain in 1997
by Hodder Children's Books

A Catalogue record for this book is available from the British Library

ISBN 0 340 68660 X

Typeset by Avon Dataset Ltd, Bidford-on-Avon, Warks

Printed and bound in Great Britain by
Clays Ltd, St Ives plc

Hodder Children's Books
a division of Hodder Headline plc
338 Euston Road
London NW1 3BH

One

Mandy Hope had just had an argument with Ross McLeod. Here they were on holiday on the beautiful island of Jura, and he'd tried to scare her with stories about a few old ghosts. 'I'm going for a look round the castle,' she called to her mother.

'With Ross?' Emily Hope called from the sitting-room at Kilmarten Lodge.

'No, by myself.' She knew he was still hanging round outside the house listening.

'Well, take care and don't be long.' They'd had a long drive from their busy vets' practice at Welford in Yorkshire, way up north to the west coast of Scotland. They'd taken a ferry from the mainland and had arrived on Jura only a few hours earlier.

'And don't talk to any strange ghosts!' her dad added. They'd already heard the local legends about Kilmarten Castle. Mary McLeod, Ross's mother, had given them a warm welcome at the lodge and entertained them with spooky stories about the last laird of the estate. He'd died on foreign soil, fighting for his country in the First World War. But he so loved his Scottish home that it was rumoured his spirit had returned here to haunt the ruins of the old castle.

As Mandy went out of the stone-built lodge into the evening sunlight, she overheard the grown-ups discussing their plans for the holiday.

'I'd love to come to the Wildlife Rescue Centre with you for a day,' Emily Hope told Mary. 'It would be good to see how you work.'

'Of course, if you're sure it's not too much of a busman's holiday for you. I thought you'd want a complete rest from work though.' Mr and Mrs Hope both worked as vets at Animal Ark. Mandy's love of animals came from them and she knew they wouldn't pass up a chance to see Mary at work.

Mary was Emily Hope's cousin; she was a gentle person with a kind smile, large grey eyes and a mass of brown curly hair. Mandy wondered how Mary had managed to have a son as rude as Ross McLeod.

Emily Hope laughed. 'We may have left Simon in charge at Animal Ark and come here for a holiday, but just try keeping me away from your place. It sounds wonderful!'

'I, on the other hand, intend to take things easy,' Adam Hope said with a yawn. 'You'll be lucky to drag me beyond the garden gate for the whole holiday!' Mandy imagined him stretching out in his chair after their big supper.

'Lazy-bones!' Mary teased.

Mandy was about to lean in through the open window and ask to join her mum on a visit to the rescue centre. She'd love to help with the animals too, like she did at home. But suddenly she saw Ross's shadow on the lawn, as his suntanned figure headed down the garden path. He was frowning and walking with his head down, his hands in his pockets. He obviously didn't think it was worth stopping to say hello to Mandy, so she let him see that she didn't care.

She ran the other way across the grass and into the woods that led to the castle. She was on Jura on holiday for two whole weeks. It was August, and the island was surrounded by sparkling waves and silver sands. The tangled forest held fallow deer, the rocky islets were home to seal colonies. For Mandy this was a wildlife paradise. And no way was Ross McLeod going to spoil that for her.

She came across the ruins of Kilmarten Castle through a wilderness of hidden paths and fallen trees, standing alone on a hill deep in shadow. Its grey stone walls rose tall and silent, covered in ivy. The windows were empty holes open to the wind and the rain.

Mandy remembered the story of the last laird and shivered. According to local legend, he still haunted these ruins. When shutters banged and stairways creaked, it was his spirit living on in the decaying rooms, looking out from the tower over his ancient forest to the lovely white shores of Selkie Bay.

Mandy stepped into the clearing from a damp, dark maze of thick bushes. The tower of the castle stood in the last rays of the evening sun. A loose shutter banged, and the pale shape of an owl rose from the turrets and flapped silently overhead.

If she hadn't promised herself not to let the stories spook her, Mandy would have turned and fled. The ruin did look ghostly, she had to admit. But the adventure of exploring inside the empty shell of the house drew her forward. Behind her in the undergrowth something scuttled. Struggling through nettles and brambles, Mandy pushed at the great wooden door. She was surprised to feel it give way to her touch. It creaked open on its rusty hinges.

Nervously she stepped inside. The floor of the main hall, once tiled, was now broken up and scattered with dead leaves. Oak-panelling on the walls was rotten, but the staircase still swept up to balconies, and the strong stone walls were intact. Looking up, Mandy could see sky through great holes in the roof, and everywhere the weather had ruined plaster-work, wooden carvings, floors and ceilings.

Mandy felt sad. If the old laird could only see his home now . . . He would see huge mirrors cracked and broken on the stairs, his hunting trophies hanging at odd angles; swords, spears and horrible animal skins. And he would see his old library shelves empty, his polished desk ruined by woodworm and rot.

Bang! went the shutter again. Mandy jumped. She had a strong feeling that she wasn't welcome here. Another bird, smaller and lighter than the owl, flitted from room to room. No, it was a bat. She shut the door quickly, but this roused others. They woke to fly in crazy patterns towards the dusk sky.

What was the legend about this place? That Murdo Kilmarten, the last laird, was so unhappy buried in a foreign field that seals from Selkie Bay swam all the way from Scotland, south to the French coast. They waited offshore and called him; six beautiful sleek grey seals. Their voices awoke the uneasily sleeping spirit of the man and it flew to join them. Together they journeyed back to Jura, where the dead man returned to his castle to finally rest in peace.

'Saved by the people of the sea,' Mary McLeod had told them. 'That's the old local name for the seals. It's a beautiful story.'

Mandy believed every word of it. She felt,

almost saw, the presence of the laird in every nook and cranny. The wind drifting through the windows disturbed the dead leaves, and there seemed to be shadows that she couldn't explain.

And footsteps.

Mandy froze. She listened again. Yes, there were footsteps on the balcony above, slow and steady, back and forth, like a man deep in thought, or reading as he paced. Any time now, a shape dressed in tartan, a grey, bearded shape in a kilt and white shirt would appear at the head of the stairs. His eyes would be hollow, his face deathly pale. There would be a bloody battle wound on his chest . . .

'Ross!' Mandy shouted out. It was Mary's son trying to scare her out of her wits. He leaned over the balcony and grinned down at her. His dark hair flopped over his forehead and the sleeves of his red-and-blue checked shirt were rolled back to the elbow. He kicked one heavy boot against the wooden balcony.

'What do you think you're doing?' Mandy asked.

'I came to see where you were.'

'No you didn't. You wanted to scare me.'

'Looks like I succeeded,' Ross said, annoyingly calm.

'No!' Mandy denied it, though her legs shook.

'You should have seen yourself jump. And I bet they heard that yell right out in the middle of the bay.' He had his mother's rolling accent, the same grey eyes. But his voice was sarcastic, his expression scornful.

By now, Mandy was angry. It was true he'd made her jump. And she didn't like being picked on for no good reason. 'What did I do?' she demanded. From the minute Ross had set eyes on her he'd gone out of his way to be unpleasant. 'Look, if you were against us coming on holiday here, you should have told your mum and stopped us. But you didn't, and here we are. So don't take it out on me!' She stood hands on hips, staring up at him. 'And if you want an argument, we'd better go outside and have the whole thing out. But not in here.' The castle belonged to the dead. They should be left in peace.

'What's wrong, you scared of ghosts?'

Mandy stared angrily, then told him the truth. 'Yes. Aren't you?'

'You're just like all the rest.' He began to make his way downstairs, kicking fallen plaster to one side, his reflection caught in jagged pieces of mirror as he came.

'Who?' Mandy stood her ground.

'All the other tourists.'

'What's wrong with that?' People could travel to Jura and fall in love with the mountains and the sea. They would want to come back again and again. There was no law against it.

'They ruin the place, that's what's wrong with it.'

'How do they?' She hadn't seen any ice-cream vans or donkeys on the beaches. There were no funfairs in Selkie Bay.

'Look, you don't understand. We just don't like our island being overrun by you lot.' Ross stood face to face with her, making it plain that he didn't want Mandy around. He was her age, but taller, skinnier. He'd obviously spent the summer out in the open air; he looked sunburned and fit.

'You're right, I don't understand. You talk about "us lot" and I don't know who you mean. All I know is that my mum is your mum's cousin. We've never visited you before, and we're only here for two weeks.' Mandy turned on her heel and walked out of the castle; she stood on the smooth, green slope overlooking the shore. 'I'm sorry if it upsets you.'

Ross seemed surprised at her quickly changing reactions. First she was scared, then angry; now she was quiet and sorry. He frowned as he followed her across the grass. He looked as if he might be ready to say sorry too.

But Mandy was too hurt to stay around where she wasn't wanted. 'The best thing I can do is to keep out of your way, OK?'

'I didn't mean—' he began. He'd gone red beneath his suntan.

'You won't have to look after me, don't worry. I don't plan to tag along after you. I'll find plenty to do by myself.' Mandy walked off towards the ancient trees growing on the slope that led to the shore. 'You don't even have to talk to me if you don't want to!'

And she left him standing by the ruined castle. She charged off through the woods in confusion, fighting through the thick laurel bushes. But however hard she tried, she couldn't forget about Ross McLeod. Just then, she came across a clearing, disturbing a small group of grazing dear.

She stood, suddenly still. The deer heard her come, but went on eating grass. Their pale yellow-brown coats, their graceful legs and straight backs were beautiful. Their eyes were large and dark as they raised their heads to glance at Mandy. The young stuck close to their mothers' sides. There were two males with magnificent antlers, and five mothers with their fawns.

The peace of the scene calmed her. At last she went on, skirting the deer's clearing, heading downhill towards the sea. There was a track to follow, mostly hidden by bushes. It led to a long finger of bare, rocky land that stretched out into the bay. Soon Mandy left the woods behind and came out into the last, low sunlight of the day. She walked along on to a spit of land into a warm breeze. To either side of the sea lapped against the rocks, and, as she looked out, the blue waves seemed to go on for ever. The wind blew Mandy's blonde hair off her face, the salt sea cleared her head of the recent trouble with Ross. And she thought again of the seals swimming to France to call their laird home to Kilmarten. Mandy listened to the waves, and thought she really *could* hear the voices of the people of the sea.

Two

A fisherman rowed a small boat across the calm water towards the shore. He made his way between the rocky islets of Selkie Bay.

Mandy already knew that 'Selkie' was an old Scottish word for 'seal', but she doubted whether she would be lucky enough to see any swimming in the sheltered waters on her first day. There were plenty of ducks at the water's edge, and even a pair of swans. They floated by the point of rocky land, grand and silent.

The fisherman landed his boat and hauled it on to the shore. Then he went up the wooded hillside and disappeared amongst the trees.

Mandy sat at the furthest point of land, staring out to sea. As the sun set, the sky turned a deep pink, and the light reflected in the calm water. Mandy guessed it was high tide, and soon time to go back to the house. But she sat on, arms clasped round her bent legs, chin resting on her knees.

The bay was scattered with small, dark rocks and islands. Her spit of land formed one edge of the bay. It ran out to sea in a straight line. But the far edge of Selkie Bay curved in the shape of a crescent moon, forming a sheltered harbour for the seabirds which she could just make out. The shore sloped more gently there, and the fringe of white looked like a fine sandy beach. But there were rocky ledges too, where the high tide lapped. To her surprise she saw more movement; smooth grey shapes sliding down the rocks, splashing into the sea. At first she wasn't sure, but then the shapes bobbed to the surface; darker, sleeker, and she could make them out as they swam lazily in her direction.

They were seals; five or six of them, slowly diving out of sight, then coming back to the surface. They swam together, nearer to

Mandy's lookout, their supple bodies twisting in the water, their strong fore-flippers steering between rocks. They would vanish below the surface, then reappear even closer to her, their heads like shiny domes, their faces whiskered, their eyes huge and dark.

Mandy didn't move. The seals drew near. They seemed to be playing a game of follow-my-leader, taking it in turns to lead. The tide carried them, and the wind was behind them. When they saw her, their bright eyes looked curious, but not afraid. They swam close to her rock, back and forth. At last one hauled himself on to dry land not thirty metres from where she sat. He'd found the last spot of sunlight in the bay, and lay there basking. Nearby, several others bobbed and swayed in the water's swell.

Mandy's seal soon dried in the sun. His fur turned from black to a pale, flecked grey. His head was raised and watchful as the others dived for fish. Then he plunged from the shore into the sea, so fast it amazed her. He too was after fish. A mother and her youngster took his place on the sunny rock. The young pup rode to shore on his mother's back and hauled himself over the rocks, full of excited curiosity.

The mother barked a warning: don't go too far. There was a stranger nearby. The pup's body scrunched up short and fat. He snuffled his nose and turned. Quickly he scrambled back to the water's edge.

The magical moments drifted on as the sun finally dipped below the horizon. The tide turned. It was time for the small seal colony to swim out to sea, back to their curved rocky shore. Mandy sighed as she watched them get ready to leave for the far side of the bay.

But they didn't swim far. They were all in the water, swimming to and fro. Were they saying goodbye to her? They bobbed close to her rock, peered up, and swam out of sight almost beneath her feet, where the rock fell away steeply. There was a drop of a few metres. The seals had gathered and stared up at her, waiting.

So Mandy climbed down to sea level. She trod carefully on the wet surface. It was slippery with seaweed, and dotted with clear rock-pools. She felt the spray on her bare legs, smelt the sharp smells of salt and sea-wrack.

The seals watched patiently. All at once, she saw what it was they seemed to want to show her. There was a seal pup stranded on a hidden ledge, just above the waterline. It was a young one, covered in thick, almost white fur, its eyes huge in its scared face. When it saw Mandy, it opened its mouth to call for its mother. The sound that came out was faint and hoarse.

Why didn't it turn away and dive into the water? Mandy wondered. Where was its mother? She'd noticed that the other pups never left their mothers' sides. But this one lay all alone, calling out with its wheezy cry. No grown-up seal came swimming to lead it out to sea. This poor baby had lost its mother, and the other seals wanted Mandy to help!

'Go on, you can do it.' Slowly she approached the abandoned pup. The waves lapped over her feet, the little seal looked up soulfully as she stopped to splash water over its back. 'The others will look after you.' She thought it might be dangerous for it to be left here alone. 'They want you to go with them.'

The pup didn't seem frightened by her gentle voice. It seemed to trust her. Carefully Mandy cupped her hands and trickled water over its soft white coat.

'Go with them. Maybe they can show you

where your mother is,' she whispered. The other seals swam in slow circles, their great eyes watching her.

The pup wriggled towards the edge of the rock. It peered into the water.

'That's it. They'll take care of you.' Somehow she knew that they wouldn't swim off and leave the lost pup. These animals seemed kind, ready to protect one another from danger.

And the pup must have thought so too. It dipped its head and snuffled at the waves, hauled itself forward on its flippers. It looked round at Mandy, who was crouched just behind. Then it made up its mind. Quickly, neatly, with hardly a splash, it plunged into the water.

Mandy heaved a sigh of relief. 'Well done, little seal!' She saw its head bob to the surface, watched as the others gathered round and guided it out to sea.

The last she saw of it was a tiny blob on the silvery surface. Seals called from the distant shore, their barks loud and sharp. 'Maybe that's where your mother is,' she murmured to the lost baby. 'Let's hope so!'

Reluctantly she turned and went back on to dry land. The woods had grown dark. The tower of Kilmarten Castle topped the trees and looked down over the shore. Quickly Mandy ran up the hill back to the lodge.

At breakfast next morning Mandy told them all about the lonely seal pup on the shore.

'That's unusual,' Mary McLeod said. Today was Sunday, a day off from her work at Jura's Wildlife Rescue Centre on the far side of the island.

Ross had left the house and gone off early without speaking to anyone. Mandy had to confess to herself that she wasn't sorry. The less she saw of her second cousin, the better, as far as she was concerned.

'I found it all by itself. I think it had lost its mother.'

Mary listened carefully. She spread honey on her toast, then asked Mandy several questions. 'How old was it?'

Mandy shook her head. 'I don't know, but it still had what I'd call its baby fur. You know, the fluffy white stuff that makes them look so sweet.'

'Lanugo,' Adam Hope announced, surprising them all by the fact that he was listening.

He was basking in the early morning sun which poured through the open french windows leading out into the garden. Just like the seals on the rocks, Mandy thought.

'That's right!' Mary smiled at him.

'Aha, we village vets don't only know about cats, dogs and hamsters, do we, Emily? I once did a special study on marine mammals off the coast of Britain.' He balanced his third cup of tea on his chest and planned a whole morning lazing in the garden. He might write a postcard to his parents back at Lilac Cottage, but nothing more exerting than that – after all, his fortnight's holiday *was* for taking things easy.

'Anyway, the baby fur, as you call it, means that the pup should definitely still be with its mother. Where did you say you spotted it?'

Mandy described the place. 'I thought the other seals would be able to take care of it,' she explained. 'They might even know where its mother is.'

'Perhaps the mother is sick or injured. That might be why the pup had to go off without her.'

Mandy hadn't thought of that. She swallowed

hard and asked the most difficult question in return. 'What will happen to the pup if the mother actually dies?'

'Or is already dead?' Mary glanced at Emily Hope. She knew that the Hopes had adopted Mandy as a baby, after Mandy's parents had been killed in a car crash.

Mandy's mum took up the explanation. 'The pup would pretty soon get very hungry. You see, it relies entirely on its mother for food until it's old enough to catch its own fish.'

'Wouldn't the others feed it?' Mandy asked.

'I'm afraid not.' Mrs Hope pushed her long auburn hair behind her ears, then leaned forward across the table to squeeze Mandy's hand. 'Let's hope for the best, though. Maybe the mother is around and can still care for her baby.'

'If not, we'll probably be able to pick it up and look after it at the rescue centre,' Mary told them briskly. 'We pass by Selkie Bay in our patrol boat every day except Sunday. We cruise around the entire island, picking up injured seabirds and seals. If a pup has been abandoned for any reason, we soon spot it. We rescue it and take it back to the centre. Then we treat it and feed it until it's ready to go back to the sea.'

Mandy nodded. 'Does that mean I did the wrong thing yesterday?' She thought now that she should have left the pup where it was and run to the lodge for help.

'No, no.' Mary was quick to reassure her. 'You did what anyone would have done; got it back into the water and swimming off towards the haul-outs. That's the rocks where the colony has its main resting places,' she explained. 'Anyway, there's no need to worry. As I said, we'll keep a special lookout in the bay during our next patrol, which will be tomorrow morning. Thanks for telling me about it, Mandy.'

And Mandy had to be satisfied with that for now. Instead of wondering about the mystery of the lone pup, she bombarded Mary with questions about their sea patrol. 'What sort of boat do you use? Where do you set out from?'

'We use a hard-bottomed inflatable with an outboard motor. It's called an Osprey Sparrow-hawk, and we set off from the rescue centre on the west coast of the island. There are two of us, Andrew Williamson and me. But we get volunteers to help us as well.' As Mandy fired questions, Mary and Emily Hope cleared the table.

'What exactly do you rescue?' She thought it sounded adventurous, setting out each day on a mission to save the wildlife of the area.

'Well, seals of course. We have to take in ones that get injured. The bull seals do each other damage during the mating season, when they're competing for females. We sew up neck wounds and give them antibiotics.'

Mandy pictured this and pulled a face. 'What else?'

'There's lots of birdlife just offshore too. Shelduck, swans, oyster-catchers. They're the ones with sharp orange beaks and a piercing cry. And then there are the diving birds; gannets, guillemots, all kinds of gulls.'

'And what happens to them?'

'We find some that can't fly. That's after they've dived through an oil slick way out at sea. Their feathers are contaminated by the oil. We have to take them in and clean them up.'

'Poor things!' Mandy had seen pictures of this on television. The birds came ashore bedraggled and covered in black oil, often too late to be saved.

'Oil is our main worry, as a matter of fact.' Mary's face grew more serious. 'It's a terrible pollutant. Even slicks far out at sea can damage the food chain. The oil contaminates the fish; then along comes a seal and eats the fish. And of course the seal if poisoned because of the oil inside the fish.'

'Does it kill the seal?'

'Sometimes. But you wouldn't believe how careless some of these oil-tankers continue to be with accidental spillages. Then of course, there's a constant danger of tankers being wrecked in a storm. We have some very fierce storms round this part of the coast, even in summer months.'

Gradually Mandy realised that wildlife rescuers didn't have such a glamorous, adventurous life after all. But she admired them even more. 'Do you go out in all weathers?'

'Rain or shine, summer or winter.' Mary smiled again. 'Would you like to come to work with me and your mum tomorrow morning?'

'You bet!' Mandy jumped at the chance.

'Good. You can meet our patients. And

Andrew, of course. Tomorrow we'll be able to tell whether Iona is well enough to come and be our guest at the lodge.'

'Who's Iona?'

'She's a grey seal. We've been treating her at the centre for the last couple of days. She has a case of lungworm, I'm afraid. But we've given her anti-worm drugs and rehydration powders. And we've been feeding her with a tube into her stomach, trying to build up her strength.'

'What does lungworm do to them?' Mandy's questions flowed on. This was all so new and interesting to her, and she always loved any new scrap of information about animals.

'The seal has difficulty breathing. But we hope Iona will be over the worst of it by tomorrow. And that means I'll be able to bring her back here to get properly better. Lots of TLC. Tender Loving Care.'

'Where would Iona stay?' It was Emily Hope's turn to wonder.

'In the bath,' Mary said, as if it was the most normal thing in the world. 'She'll play there for hours with the shower turned on.'

Adam Hope woke up from his contented snooze. He opened one eye and pretended to be shocked. 'You mean, I'll have to share a bath with a seal?'

'Or stay dirty,' Mary teased.

'Or come for a swim in the sea, Dad!' Mandy was determined to get her father to take some exercise before this holiday was over.

'No chance!' He wrinkled his nose. 'Even the thought of it sounds too energetic for my liking.'

'You can't *hear* a thought!' she told him, being deliberately fussy in order to tease him. 'A thought is silent!'

'Clever clogs.' He closed his eyes and dozed on.

'Where's Ross?' Emily Hope found Mandy on the shore and sat down beside her. It was late afternoon and they'd seen nothing of Mary's son all day. Mandy had explored the island, found new paths through the woods, seen an otter's dam across a stream and more deer amongst the hazel trees. She'd sat for ages at the sea's edge, looking for seals.

'I don't know.'

'And don't care by the sound of it?' Her mum sat on a rock and dangled her feet in the shallow water. 'Don't you two get on?'

Mandy sighed. 'It's him. He doesn't want us around. He says we spoil the island.'

'I suppose it must be a bit strange for him.'

'Why?' Mandy was used to sharing their house at Animal Ark. Visitors were always coming and going, and her grandparents popped in almost every day from their home at Lilac Cottage just down the lane.

'Mary says it's the first time they've had a family to stay with them for ages. They're pretty cut off up here, especially in the winter.'

Mandy shrugged. 'Anyway, he doesn't like me.' She remembered how he'd deliberately spooked her in the castle.

Her mum picked up white pebbles and dropped them gently into the water. I think you should make more of an effort, Mandy.'

'Why?' Surely it was up to Ross.

'Because we're his guests for a start.' Mrs Hope paused, then went on quietly. 'And because it probably is hard for Ross having us around; you, me, your dad. He's had to get used to not having his father here, and your dad must remind him of what it was like before Robert died—'

'Who was Robert?' Mandy looked up sharply.

'Ross's father. He died in a helicopter crash when Ross was eight.'

'I didn't know that.'

'No, I know you didn't. He belonged to an air-sea rescue crew on one of the oil rigs. He was killed in a storm.'

For a while Mandy stared out to sea in silence.

'I talked to Mary about it, and she said I should mention it to you. It might help to explain why Ross isn't being very friendly.' As always, Mandy's mum was kind, sensible, and perfectly truthful.

'Oh, Mum, that's awful!' She imagined losing her dad in an accident when she was old enough to realise what had happened. Old enough to miss him.

'Ross has always been a shy boy. But the accident made it worse.'

Mandy nodded. She would treat him differently from now on. She didn't know how exactly, but she was determined to be nice.

'You two do have one thing in common,' Emily Hope pointed out. She lifted her feet from the water, stood, then stooped to roll her trousers down.

'What's that?' So far, Mandy hadn't seen how she could possibly hit it off with Ross McLeod.

'Animals.'

'You mean he likes them?'

'Loves them, according to Mary. He goes out on patrol as a volunteer. She says that what he doesn't know about seals isn't worth knowing. And this spring he hand-reared some orphan swallows in a heated box in his bedroom. There were three babies, and two survived. Mary says she's never seen anyone with such patience with animals as Ross.'

Mandy stood up too. She shook her head in amazement. 'Patience? Ross McLeod?'

'Yes. So if you want to break down some barriers, try your own favourite subject, Mandy Hope! Otters, voles, fallow deer, eider ducks, swans, seal colonies . . . If you stop to think, the two of you have plenty to talk about after all!'

Three

'Are you sure this was the place?' Ross followed
Mandy along the long spit of rock where she'd
seen the baby seal the night before. She had
managed to persuade Ross to come and help
her find the seal pup by reminding him that
there was no rescue patrol on a Sunday. She'd
gone straight off to find him after her talk with
her mum.

'Yes, right there.' Mandy pointed to the spot.
She had even made sure to bring him out here
at evening high tide, so everything was the
same as the night before.

'Well, it's not come back tonight,' Ross said

abruptly. The way he said it made it sound like he didn't believe it had been there in the first place.

Mandy stood helpless and frustrated. She looked out over Selkie Bay. 'What if the pup was an orphan? It must be pretty hungry by now. By tomorrow it might have starved to death.' She was serious about this. The more she thought about the baby seal, the more anxious she grew.

Ross frowned stubbornly at the empty rock. 'Well, it's not here, is it?'

'No, but couldn't we take one of those boats out and have a proper look?' She pointed to the four small wooden rowing-boats that lay hauled up on the pebble beach. They lay in a row, hulls upturned; two white, one green, one red. 'You brought that food with you, didn't you?'

'Liquidised herring.' He nodded. 'But I can't give it to an invisible seal, can I?' He turned to scan the bay. 'The colony isn't on its haul-outs tonight, so where do you suggest we row to?'

Ross hadn't grown any friendlier since Mandy had come across him sitting on Castle Hill, whittling away at a piece of wood with a sharp knife. He'd only agreed to come because she'd spent so much time explaining that she thought the mother must have abandoned the pup.

'We could try some of these tiny islands in the bay.' She refused to give in. If seals were creatures of habit, she guessed that the same small colony that had adopted the pup the night before would be somewhere close by.

'Can you row a boat?' he demanded.

'Yes.' She looked him in the eye, not letting on that she'd only ever been in one three times in her life, and never at sea.

Ross stared back. 'Well, I suppose we could take a look.'

Mandy nodded. 'Right, come on then.' She headed for the boats. 'Which one can we use?'

'The green one. That belongs to the lodge.' Ross told her to take the weight of the small boat and help him to turn it over. 'Grab that edge. Ready; one, two, three!'

Together they righted the boat and dragged it to the water's edge. Then Ross ran back for the oars and told Mandy to sit on the bench in the stern. 'I'll row to start off with. You keep a lookout.' He waded into the sea, pushing the boat with Mandy sitting in it. Then, once it was afloat, he slung his canvas fishing-bag into the bottom and hopped in to take his place at the oars.

The boat rocked, then steadied. Ross began to row with a steady rhythm. The oars dipped underwater, and reappeared gleaming and dripping. He made hardy any splash as he sliced them back into the waves, rowing against the tide easily and strongly.

After a while Mandy got used to being afloat. They rowed through seaweed and eelgrass into clearer water. She sat in the stern feeling the fresh breeze tug her hair back from her face, looking out for any sign of the seals.

Ross rowed on in silence. They went between rocks, round islets, sometimes pulled or pushed by strong currents. The sea was green and crystal-clear. But the only signs of life were the great grey-and-white gulls perched on the dark rocks, and the swooping shelducks as they came in to land.

'Could we try and tempt the seals with some fish?' Mandy asked. If they could draw some near to the boat, there might be a chance of spotting her pup.

'Not until we see some.' Ross took a look behind him, over the prow of the boat. 'See that island up ahead? It's called Chapel Rock. It's where the people of the sea sit and call to the laird in his castle.'

The rocky island sat in the green water, a long, low pyramid. A few small clouds hung over it in a mostly clear sky. Mandy refused to react to this strange tale about a dead man and his mysterious 'people'. 'Let's try there then,' she said, matter-of-factly. 'If that's where the seals like to gather, that's where we should look next.'

Ross altered course to do as she said. 'See the stone cross on the island? And the chapel ruins?' he asked.

'Yep.' The cross stood on the hilltop, silhouetted against the sky. Nearby were the ruins of a small building with arched windows.

'Well, that's the old chapel. It's haunted too.'

'Really?' Mandy intended to ignore the warning. 'Look, I can see seals!' Her voice rose in excitement. Two of them swam amongst snaking fronds of eelgrass, circling each other, minding their own business. 'Never mind if it's haunted; shall I get the fish out of the bag?'

He grinned. 'Not scared this time?'

'Course not.'

'Not even if I say it's haunted by all the ghosts of the seal hunters who used to cull the pups up and down this coast? People say they get turned back at the gates of heaven and they're sent here until the seals choose to forgive them. There's no way on or off the island, see. So no one knows how the chapel was built, or who used it. They say it's a prison for dead spirits.'

The two seals slowly glided towards their boat. 'Serves them right.' Mandy was still down-to-earth. 'Come on, Ross, give them something to eat!'

He stared hard at her, then rested the oars. Leaning forward, he took a plastic box from the bag in the bottom of the boat. 'This is sliced herring, not the liquidised stuff,' he told her. 'We'd better save that for the pup, in case we ever find it.' He took the lid off the box and handed it to Mandy. 'Go ahead, then.'

So Mandy took a piece of slippery fish and tossed it into the sea. The two seals surged towards it, twisted and plunged after it. They came up for more, pink mouths wide open, heads stretching towards the boat. She threw more fish for them to eat. 'They're not afraid of us, are they?'

Ross shook his head. 'They're used to me. Watch this.' Taking some fish from the box, he held it high in the air. One of the seals came up and made a neat jump to nip the fish out of his hand. When it landed, it came up to him for a pat of congratulation. 'Nice one!' Ross scratched its round, sleek head and watched it swim off.

'They're like dolphins!' Mandy was breathless with wonder.

'Better!' he insisted. 'Have you got your swimming things on?'

She nodded. 'Why?'

'You can go in and swim with them if you want.'

'Seriously; you mean it?' She peered into the deep water, watching the pair of seals circle round their boat.

'I do it all the time.' It was Ross's turn to be matter-of-fact.

So Mandy took her first chance to go into the water with these marvellous creatures. She took off her T-shirt and slipped into the cold depths, felt her skin tingle and took a sharp

breath. Then she swam a few strokes. The seals
came up to her. Full of curiosity, they dived
beneath her, then came up so close that she
could touch them. They paddled with their
flippers, rolled on to their backs, showed
her how to dive under the boat and come up
the other side. As she got used to them swimming within arm's reach, Mandy studied their
streamlined bodies, and laughed at their
whiskery faces and black snub-noses. 'This is
brilliant!' she called to Ross, still sitting in the
boat.

'Not too cold for you?'

'No. Why not come in?' She floated on her
back, looking up at the sky.

'Not now. We'd better carry on looking if we
want to find this pup.' He glanced back at the
sun setting behind them.

Mandy had been swimming with the seals
for longer than she'd realised. Now she saw
that she and Ross would have to row away from
the haunted isle, to go on with their search.
She pulled herself back into the boat from the
stern end while Ross kept his weight at the bow.
Soon they were waving goodbye to the friendly
pair.

'Let me row this time,' Mandy offered. 'It'll get me warm again.' She'd pulled on her T-shirt, but her skin was still damp.

'OK,' Ross agreed. He watched her take up the oars, but said nothing as she struggled to use them as she'd seen him do.

The oars twisted in her hands, and hit the water flat, instead of slicing through like a blade. 'I'm not very good at this, am I?' she said with a frown.

Ross grinned and shook his head. He didn't lose his patience, but showed her a better way to do it. 'Head for home,' he told her at last. 'I don't think we're going to find your pup out this way. We'll probably have to leave it to the patrol boat tomorrow.'

Mandy was disappointed, but she was forced to agree.

'At least we tried,' Ross said, more kindly than she'd expected. He offered to row again, now that they drew closer to the shore. 'I'll steer us safely in,' he explained.

So they changed places once more, and Mandy sat quietly in the stern as they passed the finger of rock where she'd first seen the seals. This evening it was deserted. Or was it?

She looked again. There, on the same ledge where the baby had been stranded, was a movement; a raised head, a tiny, hoarse cry.

'Ross!' Mandy whispered a warning for him to stop rowing. She pointed to the ledge, not wanting to frighten the young seal away. 'It's come back!'

He saw it straight away. It had raised its head, but seemed helpless to shift from the rock. The tide was turning, beginning to ebb. Soon the pup would be stranded once more.

'Exactly the same as last night!' Mandy breathed. 'It's come back to the very same spot!' There was still no mother to be seen, and this time no friendly seal colony to help it.

'It looks to me like it's in trouble,' Ross said. He made an instant decision to approach by boat. They changed course and headed for the rock.

'It's tangled in a mass of seaweed!' Mandy watched the pup struggle to free its body from the thick eelgrass.

'That's OK, don't panic. At least it means it can't try to move off before we get there. We'll be able to get a good look at it.' Ross steered the boat right up to the rock. 'I'll stay here in the boat. I'll have to use the oars to stay close. I won't drift far.'

'Is this what you want me to do?' She stood up, ready to jump from the boat on to the low ledge.

'Yes, go ahead. Tell me what you see.'

Mandy took a leap and landed safely. She went over to the seal. 'She can hardly breathe,' she reported. 'I think she's very sick now!'

'Is she trying to escape?'

'No. She's trying to make a noise, but it's coming out wheezy.' Mandy listened to the hoarse call. She saw the pup lower its head and wait for help. Behind her, Ross struggled to keep the boat bobbing at a safe distance from the rocks.

'We'll have to get her back to the lodge,' he called. 'She needs urgent treatment.' His voice was tense.

Mandy bent over the struggling pup and tried to untangle the eelgrass from its tail.

'Let's try to get her into the boat and row her to the shore. It'll be quickest.' Ross was the one making the decisions. He was calm enough to think it through.

'How?' Mandy almost panicked as she realised how sick the pup must be. 'What's wrong with her, Ross?'

'It sounds like lungworm. Come on, Mandy, I've brought the boat in as close as I can.'

At last she managed to free the pup. But still she had to struggle to lift her. The pup was small, but solid and heavy. Mandy picked her up and carried her to the water's edge. 'Closer if you can!' she shouted.

Ross used the oars to squeeze the boat between two rocky outcrops. He steered into the tight space, and saw that he could lean out with one hand and grab on to one rock. 'I'll hold it steady while you bring the pup on board!' he called to Mandy.

'Keep still!' Mandy gasped with the effort of freeing the trapped animal and carrying it struggling to the water. 'Hold on; I'm coming in!' She took a wide step from rock to boat, holding the pup in her arms.

The boat lurched and rocked sideways. Mandy kept her balance, feeling the waves splash in around her ankles. She gave a little cry.

'It's OK, you made it. Put her in the bottom

here.' Ross watched Mandy lay the sick pup in the pool of salt water at their feet.

'Quick, Ross. Let's get her home as fast as we can!'

He picked up the oars and rowed.

Four

The seal lay miserably in the bottom of their boat. Her breathing was wheezy, her head lolled in the puddle of sea-water.

'How is she?' Mandy bent to try and stroke her, but the pup turned to try and nip her hand.

'Pretty bad. She only looks about three or four weeks old, but she's underweight; only about fourteen kilos.'

'How are we going to carry her all the way to the lodge?'

Ross thought fast as he brought the boat around the narrow headland towards the sheltered shore. 'In this!' He stopped rowing to pull off his checked shirt, ready to turn it into a sling. 'We'll have to shuffle her on to it, then pick it up by the corners and carry her.'

Mandy agreed with the plan. She felt the boat scrape against the shore. Then she jumped out and helped Ross to drag it on to dry land.

They lay the shirt in the bottom of the boat. Mandy tempted the seal pup forward with a handful of the mashed herring that Ross had brought. Though she was sick and weak, the smell of food drew her on to the shirt. It was wringing wet, but tough. It would make a perfect makeshift sling. Mandy tied the sleeves around the pup's body to keep her firmly in place, then she and Ross each grabbed two corners and lifted.

'OK?' Ross asked as they took the weight.

Mandy nodded. 'Let's go.'

So they lifted her clear of the boat and headed for the lodge.

Mary McLeod took one look at the pup and confirmed a case of lungworm. 'She'll need two types of antibiotic and an anti-worm drug.' She said. 'There's this small infected wound on her back flipper as well as the infection in the lungs.' Luckily Mary had both types of medicine to hand.

She, Emily and Adam Hope had come running to meet Ross and Mandy when they saw them struggling out of Castle Wood with their injured patient. Everyone stayed calm. Adam told Mandy not to worry; the pup was in good hands. They'd taken her quickly into the house. Mary decided to administer the antibiotics in fluid form, using a stomach tube.

'Just tell us what to do,' Adam Hope told Mary. 'You're the seal expert. We'll do what we can to help.'

Mary told Mandy and Ross to bring the pup straight into the downstairs bathroom. 'Fill the bath with lukewarm water,' she told Mandy. Then she asked Emily Hope to hold the pup firmly on the floor. 'We have to insert the tube down her mouth right into the stomach,' she told Mr Hope. 'Can you ease her mouth open while I slide the tube in?'

The pup struggled but was unable to resist. Mandy kept busy at the taps. She felt better when she had something useful to do.

'Ross, I'll need a packet of rehydration powder from my bag in the car.' Mary also named the drugs she needed and asked him to fetch them at the same time.

'What's the powder for?' Mandy saw the clear tube slide down the seal's throat, and watched as Mary fitted a small funnel on to the end.

'It's glucose and body salts. It will help to normalise the pup's fluid levels. I want you to mix it with water, Mandy. Use that plastic jug on the shelf behind you.'

As soon as Ross ran back with the medicines, Mandy did as she was asked. Then she handed the jug to Mary, who tipped the liquid slowly into the funnel with a steady hand.

'OK, everyone?' she asked as the last drop disappeared. 'We can relax now.'

Mandy's mum waited until Mr Hope had removed the tube, then she let the pup wriggle free. 'Well done, you two,' she told Ross and Mandy. 'It looks like you found her in the nick of time.'

'You'd better thank Mandy,' Ross mumbled. 'She was the one who took me out looking. I wouldn't have gone if it wasn't for her.'

'Thanks, both of you,' Adam Hope insisted.

'And don't just hang about looking embarrassed,' Mary cut in. 'Here's some cream to put on that wound on her flipper. Then the two of you can put her in the bath.'

'Will she be OK now?' Mandy went to hold the pup's head, while Ross rubbed some antiseptic cream on to the flipper.

'Let's hope so. We'll soon be able to tell.' Mary was satisfied with what they'd done. She dried her hands on a towel and stood back beside Mandy's mum and dad. 'But she'll need round the clock care for the first twenty-four hours. I wonder who we can get to do that?'

'I will!' Ross and Mandy said in the same split

second. Then they grinned sheepishly at each other.

'It's a team effort, then,' Adam Hope said cheerfully.

Together they lifted the pup into the warm bath. She seemed to sigh. Then she wallowed and at last peered at them over the edge.

'She likes it!' Mandy was delighted to see the pup splashing about. She'd stopped squirming and struggling and no longer seemed sluggish. The change had been magically quick.

'Let me tell you what you'll have to do to nurse her.' Mary didn't want Mandy to think it would be plain sailing. 'You'll have to give her four or five feeds of the glucose mixture in the first day, in a baby's bottle. You'll be checking her temperature all this time. After the first twenty-four hours, you'll add liquidised herring to the glucose mix. She should begin to put on some weight. Then, when she can chew and swallow properly, you can give her the herring in small slices.'

'How long for?' To Mandy this sounded great. At home at Animal Ark she was used to helping nurse many of her parents' patients back to health in the residential unit behind the surgery. But this would be the first time she had taken so much responsibility on her own. It made her feel that she was one step nearer to becoming a real vet; the third in the Hope family.

'A few days. After that, we'll see. In fact, let's get through the first night, shall we? Then we can look a bit further ahead.' Mary took a last look at the patient, then left them to it.

'You realise you won't be able to come to the rescue centre tomorrow?' Emily Hope popped back into the bathroom to remind Mandy. 'And that's supposed to be your first real treat of the holiday.'

Ross stepped in. 'It's OK, you go. I'll stay here and look after this one,' he offered. It was kindly meant.

Mandy blushed. 'No, it's OK, thanks. I'd rather stay here and help you.' There would be other times to go and see Mary's official patients.

'You organise it between you, then.' Emily Hope smiled to herself and went off.

'It looks like we're in charge,' Ross said.

'No, *you* are,' said Mandy. 'You've done this loads of times before, and I haven't.'

'OK, then. We have to barricade her in the bath in case she tries to get out. We'll need some kitchen chairs.'

Mandy went and brought them in one at a time.

'Now, we should make up plenty of glucose mix, and we have to sterilise the tube and funnel.' Ross ticked things off on his fingers.

'When will she need her next feed?'

'In six hours. That'll be about two in the morning. You don't have to stop up if you don't want to.'

'I do,' Mandy answered promptly. 'Anyway, it'll take two of us to do it properly.'

'OK, if you don't mind.' The seal pup was peering over the edge of the bath at them, calm and attentive, as if she was listening to their plan. Ross smiled at her. 'What do you want to call her?' he asked Mandy.

Ross was full of nice surprises, ever since they'd been out in the boat and she'd swum with the seals. 'You want me to choose?' she asked.

'Sure. You rescued her.'

Mandy felt herself blush again. 'Let's see, what would be a good name?'

'Choose a nice one.' Ross went over and

stroked the little seal. His dark hair fell forward over his grey eyes, his voice was low and gentle. The pup looked up at him with her enormous eyes.

'Selkie,' Mandy decided at last. 'Something plain and simple. What do you think?'

'It suits her,' Ross said. He turned to talk gently to the pup. 'Little Selkie. That's your name from now on.'

Selkie took her feed at two in the morning. Mandy and Ross lifted her gently out of the bath and put her down on to a towel. She struggled less than before as she took the bottle. Soon she sucked strongly, seeming to know that her carers only did what was good for her. When they put her back into fresh water, Mandy was amazed to see that she lay flat and sank to the bottom. Soon she was completely submerged.

'What's she doing?'

'Sleeping,' Ross replied.

'Underwater?'

He stood by the bath watching. 'She comes up every few minutes to breathe. It's called "bottling".'

It was the first of many seal facts that Mandy learned. She watched Ross take Selkie's temperature and announce that it was dropping to normal. Mandy could see the improvement. By morning, Selkie was breathing easily.

All next day, while Emily Hope and Mary McLeod went off to the rescue centre, Mandy and Ross stayed at Kilmarten Lodge to clean, bathe and feed the pup. Mandy got used to running warm water into the bath, mixing in some disinfectant and lifting Selkie back in. She watched her suck her flippers, heard her sigh with pleasure as they lifted her out and dried her with a towel until she was white and fluffy. Mandy was amazed when Ross said that Selkie was allowed out of the bathroom into the rest of the house.

'Won't your mum mind?'

He shook his head. 'We're used to it in this house. You'll have to watch it though; Selkie's latched on to you!'

They laughed as the little pup flopped out into the corridor and followed Mandy into the kitchen.

'She's just like a dog!'

'Better!' Ross gave his usual reply. 'She'll follow you everywhere you go if you're not careful. She'll sit and watch TV with you, or come out into the garden. She won't let you out of her sight.'

'Great!' It really did seem to be true. Selkie's little flippers flapped over the cold tiled floor. She stretched her neck up to Mandy and waved her tail in the air. 'Why me?' Mandy asked.

'She knows you saved her life,' Ross said. He went to make a giant cheese sandwich for his lunch, and told Mandy to help herself. 'I suppose Selkie follows you because she trusts you,' he said thoughtfully. 'Seals are like that. Once they find someone they like, they never forget them.'

By day three, a Wednesday, their worries for Selkie's health had lifted. Janet declared the pup fully fit. Selkie gobbled up every scrap of sliced herring they could lay their hands on.

And she didn't need the bottle any more. Instead, she drank from a bowl and fed on slices of fish from Mandy's hand. The wound on her flipper had healed and her eyes gleamed.

'She's losing her baby fur,' Mandy remarked as she and Ross took Selkie down through the woods to the beach for the first time. She was shedding it surprisingly quickly.

'The white lanugo will fall out and show her real colouring. It's probably a pale speckled grey,' Ross explained.

They were taking Selkie to the beach to let a new visitor to the lodge settle in. Mary had come home that evening with Iona, her patient from the centre. Iona had been slower to recover from her illness, but now she was almost ready to be released into the sea once more. She was in the bath at the lodge right now, nose resting on the silver taps, flippers flapping gently in the lukewarm water.

'Do you think Selkie will mind Iona taking over the bathroom?' Mandy wondered. They arrived at the beach and sat down, waiting until the pup scrunched up her body and settled down on the warm pebbles.

'A bit. But it'll soon be time for Selkie to be on her way in any case.'

The words went through Mandy like an electric shock. Of course she knew that all wild animals must go back to their natural surroundings, that it was cruel to keep them in captivity. But she hadn't had time to get used to the idea of parting with Selkie just yet. 'Just like that?' she pleaded. Ross had sounded offhand, as if he suddenly didn't care.

He stood up and went to skim flat pebbles along the surface of the water. 'It'll take a while yet, don't worry.'

'How long?' Stupidly she'd dreamed that Selkie would be with them right up to the end of their holiday. She loved hearing the pup follow her through the house. Selkie would come up for tidbits at the table, snuggling beside her as the evenings drew in.

'I'm not sure. She'll start going for a swim soon. Maybe tomorrow.'

Mandy held back a gasp of surprise. So soon?

'But she'll keep coming back until she's really ready. She'll begin to spend more and more time in the water. Eventually she'll stop coming back altogether.' He accepted that it would happen like this. It always did.

'Maybe she'll stick around until we leave?' Mandy said hopefully. They had a week and a half left to spend on Jura.

He shrugged. 'Who knows? Anyway, it's better if they don't stay too long. They need to be free.'

'Oh, I know that,' Mandy said hastily. But she watched sadly as Selkie roused herself and shuffled down to the water to join Ross.

'End of August,' he said quietly. 'That's when seal pups leave their mothers. The young ones go off together.'

'And they can look after themselves from then on?' It seemed so soon to face the open sea.

'If people leave them alone, they can.' Suddenly, all Ross's calmness slipped away. 'But that's the trouble, they don't.'

He was back to the Ross she first knew; angry and fierce. His smooth, brown face creased into a frown.

'Even the sea,' he told her. 'They can't even leave the sea alone. There's a mystery virus now that attacks whole colonies of seals, did you know that? And no one knows where it's come from, so they can't find a cure. And then there's oil-tankers and all other kinds of pollution.' He flung the pebbles down, turned on his heel and left Selkie stranded by the shallow waves.

Mandy went to crouch beside her. 'But not on purpose,' she said. Ross had wandered off, turned his back on them. 'No one pollutes the sea on purpose.'

'Want to bet?' He rounded on her. 'What about these giant oil rigs? If you really want to know, that's who I hate! They just grab what they want, no matter what it does to the wildlife that really belongs here!' He spoke bitterly. 'I don't think they should be allowed!'

As he stamped away, head down, angrier than she'd ever seen him, Mandy could see why. His father; that was it. Robert McLeod had worked on an oil rig. To Ross it must look as if the oil company had robbed him of his father. Now Ross fought to protect seals and seabirds from the effects of the oil. No wonder he was bitter.

Mandy stayed on the shore with Selkie long after Ross had stormed off up Castle Hill. She looked out over the calm, clear waters. There were no seals out there tonight, and the only movement was in the waves and the slow drift of clouds overhead. The sea shone like melted gold in the late sun. As she gazed across the bay, Mandy thought of Ross's angry warnings. But she saw only a safe haven for the seal pup in the sheltered waters of Selkie Bay.

Five

Next morning, however, there was a sad sign that Ross McLeod might well have been right.

It was Mandy who was up early and on the shore at Selkie Bay. She'd gone there just after dawn to buy herring from the fisherman who rowed out to sea twice daily. He went out to the fishing-grounds beyond the sheltered bays and islands at high tide every day. Since she'd started looking after Selkie, Mandy had made sure she was first on the beach when he brought in his early morning catch.

'Hi, Gordon!' She ran barefoot into the water to help him heave the boat on to dry land. She

liked the weather-beaten old man in his battered cagoul and big wellingtons. His voice was
a low growl, his long white moustache reminded her of a walrus, and his eyes were almost
hidden behind wrinkled eyelids and bushy
eyebrows. But he was always pleased to see her
and ready with a tale of the seals at their haul-
outs; how two had followed him out to sea
leaping like porpoises, or how they had circled
his boat and popped up for the tiddlers which
he had thrown back into the sea.

'Hello, Amanda.' He hauled his boat over
the pebbles then laid his oars safely inside. 'By
yourself, I see?' He looked round for Ross.

Gordon was the only person who called
Mandy by her full name. Somehow she didn't
mind. 'I was up early. I'm going to the Wildlife
Rescue Centre today,' she said. This would be
the first time she'd dared to leave Selkie since
she and Ross had rescued her. Ross had been
quiet since their talk about the oil companies.
After supper he'd kept to himself and wandered off alone through Castle Wood. Today
he'd decided to stay at Kilmarten Lodge with
Selkie while the others went with Mary to the
rescue centre.

Gordon nodded. 'Isn't that a lucky thing?' He peered into the boat from behind his shaggy brows.

'Is it?' She looked at the heap of silver fish, at the fishing-nets and gear that Gordon used. There was a tarpaulin scrunched up at the far end of the small boat.

'It is for this wee thing.' He bent to turn back one corner of the tarpaulin. 'I found him out there on the water. He was in a bad way. Now you can take him up to the lodge for me. Then Mary McLeod can drive him to the centre to see if there's anything they can do.'

Mandy peeped under the heavy canvas sheet. She hardly knew what to expect. Another seal pup abandoned by its mother, perhaps? These days her mind was so fixed on Selkie that she wasn't prepared for what she actually saw.

'Can you get at him?' Gordon eased the tarpaulin away from the corner.

Mandy gasped. A bird struggled in the bottom of the boat. It was large; bigger than a blackbird, as big as a rook or a raven, with a long neck and a grey beak. It spread its wings in a feeble attempt to fly, but had to sink exhausted into the bottom of the boat. 'What's wrong with him?' She turned in alarm to the fisherman.

'Oil,' he said simply. 'It's all over his feathers, see!'

She looked more closely. This bird wasn't black after all. Its natural colour must be white or grey. But it was coated in a thick, tarry liquid. 'What happened?'

'I didn't see exactly. I just spotted him out there and brought him in. With a bit of luck he won't have swallowed any contaminated fish, but he certainly dived into a big patch of oil somewhere out there, and this is the result.' Gordon's voice was edged with disgust at the mess the oil had made of the poor bird.

Mandy saw its head sink down in exhaustion. It battered its wings against the wooden hull. 'How long ago?' She edged forward, ready to fold its wings against its sides and pick it up with both hands.

'I can't say. I didn't see the oil slick, though, so he must have been struggling to stay afloat for quite a while. Of course, he can't fly; not with his feathers in this terrible state. He can't fish, and the cold gets in through the oily feathers. He's certainly in no condition to look after himself.'

Gently Mandy folded the bird's wings and cupped her hands beneath him. He pecked weakly at her fingers. 'What sort of bird is it?'

'Guillemot. Easy does it.' He watched Mandy hold the bird to her chest. 'That's it, keep him warm. Get him up to the lodge as quickly as you can. Your legs can run faster than mine. Tell them I'll call in with their fish as I'm passing. Go on, off you go!'

So Mandy sped up the beach. The poor guillemot could only put up a weak protest. It

opened its long beak, gave a cry, and wriggled its head and neck, but found itself firm in her grasp. The oil covered it from head to foot in a slimy black coating, greasy to the touch.

She ran through the thick maze of Castle Wood, over the hill to the lodge. The first person she saw there was Ross. 'Quick, fetch your mum!' Mandy called. There wasn't a second to be lost.

Ross spotted the problem and ran inside the house without a word. By the time Mandy reached the door, Mary, Ross and her dad were ready and waiting. From the lawn by the french windows Selkie and Iona sat and watched, heads raised, eyes alert.

'Bring him into the bathroom!' Mary led the way. 'Ross, we need you, quickly!' This was a familiar sight; an oiled bird needing intensive care if they were to save its life.

Once more the McLeods' bathroom was turned into an animal hospital. Mary explained that they must help the bird by giving him lectade through a tube down his throat. 'It's like the drip a doctor would attach to a human patient suffering from shock or dehydration,' Mary said. 'The oil makes them lose body fluid.' She was calm and worked quickly.

'What about its feathers?' Mandy was still gasping for breath after her sprint up the hill.

'We'll deal with that later, at the rescue centre. That's when we clean him up with a dispersant to get rid of the oil. And we just hope he hasn't ingested any of it.'

Mandy looked at her dad. 'Will he be OK?'

'It's fifty-fifty,' he said quietly. 'The oil's highly toxic. If he's swallowed some, it doesn't look good.'

'But we'll try?' Mandy saw how much the bird was suffering. Its beautiful grey feathers were clogged with crude oil; it shivered from shock and cold.

'We'll do our best.' Mary had finished with the tube and wrapped the oiled bird in a towel. 'Come on, it's only a twenty minute drive across the island to the centre. Do you think you can manage?' She handed the patient to Mandy, who nodded. 'Good. Hop in the car.'

'I'll follow with Emily in ours,' Adam Hope suggested. 'You get moving. We won't be long.'

'And I'll stay here and take care of Selkie,' Ross promised. He knew Mandy would worry about the seal pup.

'Gordon will bring their breakfast!' she called from the car. 'Hers and Iona's!' She could see the two seals still staring curiously from the front lawn. But there was no time to say good-bye as Mary slammed the car into gear and set off across the island.

The road was wild and winding, over a bleak mountain pass and down again to the west coast, to another bay fringed with rock and white pebbles.

'Nearly there!' Mary pointed to some simple, low, wooden huts standing at the water's edge. There was a grey inflatable boat by a jetty, and two Land-rovers parked by the huts. At the door of one of them, a man stood waiting. 'There's Andrew. Ross must have telephoned with the news.'

They pulled up by the rescue centre and Mandy carried the guillemot inside. By now it lay still in her arms; only its eyes gave any sign of life. She hoped and prayed that they weren't too late.

Once inside, Andrew Williamson showed her how to clean the oil from the bird's feathers. They wore thick rubber gloves and began gently to wipe a dispersant liquid on to the wings. It had to be done softly, and it would take many hours to clean the feathers completely. 'A little at a time,' Andrew explained. 'He needs to recover from the shock, but bit by bit we should be able to get him back on his feet.' He and Mary left Mandy to work on the wings, while they discussed the bird's chances.

'It looks like shock, not ingested oil,' Mary said. She brought a cage down from a high shelf for the bird to rest in.

'Thank goodness.' Andrew seemed to agree. He was a small, sandy-haired man in his twenties, dressed in a tweedy roll-neck jumper and jeans. 'At least he stands a better chance if he hasn't swallowed any.' He heard the story from Mary of how Gordon MacRae had discovered the bird at sea and handed him over to Mandy in Selkie Bay. 'I'll get on to the coast-guard again. They might send a helicopter over the area to check for oil. Perhaps they can see which way the slick is heading.'

He went to make the call while Mandy and Mary put the bird into the cage. By now the worst of the oil was off, but his feathers were still stained dark brown. He looked bedraggled and sorry for himself as he peered out from behind the wire bars.

Mary nodded and stood back. 'That's all we can do for now. Come on, if you like, I'll show you round.'

Mandy glanced down at her oil-stained T-shirt. She took off the rubber gloves and threw them into a waste bin. Now she noticed the other seabirds ranged in cages along the work-bench. They watched quietly, feathers clean and soft, chests puffed out. 'Were they all brought in like the guillemot?' she asked.

'Mostly. We find oiled birds much too often when we're out on patrol, I'm afraid. But there have been even more than usual in the last few days. We rescued seven. Of those, we lost three and saved four.'

Mandy peered into the cages. 'Does anyone know where the oil's coming from?'

Mary shook her head. 'No, we rarely find the culprits. That's part of the problem. There are so many oil-tankers up and down the west coast of Scotland, and the tides can carry the slicks an awful long way. Until a coastguard can spot it from a helicopter there's no way of knowing even how big it is, let alone which way it might be heading.'

She led Mandy into the other, bigger hut. It had a corrugated plastic roof that let in the light, but it was the smell of fish and salt water that hit Mandy first. Then she saw the metal tanks full of water, and inside the tanks the round, shiny heads of the island creatures she loved best of all. 'Seals!' she cried.

'And all on the road to recovery, fortunately.' Mary smiled. She introduced Mandy to their patients; a bull seal with an eye infection, another with a torn front flipper, a young female who had been a victim of the oil. 'We found her out in the fishing-grounds north of Jura the day before yesterday. There were oil toxins in her stomach, which means she'd eaten polluted fish. Luckily, we could treat her in time.'

Mandy frowned. 'Why can't we do anything to stop the oil?'

'You sound like Ross,' Mary told her. 'That's what he always asks. And it's a big question without an answer, I'm afraid.'

Just then Andrew came back with news from the coastguard. 'He says they've pinpointed the slick at last,' he reported. 'It's a couple of hundred metres long and about fifty wide.'

To Mandy this sounded enormous. A big black stain on the beautiful clear sea.

'The wind's carrying it north of the strait between Jura and Islay, well away from us at the moment.'

Mary nodded and looked at Mandy. 'Don't worry. It's not such a big one. And if the wind stays in the west, it should steer clear of us.'

'And if not?' She didn't like to think the worst, but she wanted to know what the dangers were.

'Well, if it changes direction and heads this way, we have an emergency on our hands,' Andrew admitted. 'Everything in the sea is at risk from an oil spillage, from the smallest crustaceans and starfish, right through the food chain, including shrimp, worms, fish, up to the seabirds and seals you've just seen.'

Mandy looked round at the seals happily wallowing in their tanks. They peered over the sides, whiskers dripping, noses snuffling for food. They opened their pink mouths, yawned or barked. She felt a surge of helpless anger. 'It shouldn't be allowed!' she protested, following Andrew and Mary out into the fresh air.

They stood on the jetty, checking the direction of the wind, gazing at a bank of clouds which sat low on the horizon.

Mary rested an arm on Mandy's shoulder. 'Now you really do sound like Ross,' she said with a gentle smile.

'Seals are amazing animals. Did you know, they can live up to thirty years?' Ross said.

Mandy was back at Kilmarten Lodge after an exciting day helping out at the rescue centre. She'd cleaned out seal tanks, disinfected them, filled them with fresh water. She'd been on patrol, right around the island in the Sparrowhawk inflatable boat. They'd chugged quietly between the islands, down the strait of water which separated Jura from neighbouring Islay.

She'd even seen Selkie Bay from the seals' angle; a calm, semicircular bay fringed with rocky headlands. The rocks made perfect haul-outs for resting seals, and she'd been lucky enough to spot several small colonies.

Now she was back home, sitting on the edge of the bath, tired out but happy, watching Ross play Selkie's favourite game. He turned on the shower and sprayed it all over her. 'Thirty years,' he repeated. 'That's how long a seal can live.'

'And does each seal have its own special markings?' Mandy smiled as Selkie opened her mouth wide and let the shower sprinkle over her face.

'Yes, you never see two the same. They have different colours, markings, shapes; everything. Some are sandy coloured with white splodges, some are nearly white, or nearly black; it depends.' He sprayed Selkie's grey speckled coat.

'Can you recognise any of them by sight?'

'Most of the ones with haul-outs in Selkie Bay. I've given them all names,' he confessed. 'There's Melody and Sunbeam, Misty and Shadow. I can tell them all apart. Then of course there's Gordon . . .'

'Gordon?' Mandy interrupted.

'He's an old seal with white whiskers.' Ross's eyes twinkled. He ran the spray along the length of Selkie's back.

'Like Gordon the fisherman?' Mandy laughed.

Ross grinned. 'Don't tell him. He wouldn't think it was funny!'

Mandy swung her legs over the side of the

bath to kick her feet in the water. Soon Selkie was flapping her flippers in reply. There seemed to be a smile on her face and she gave happy little grunts as she splashed and played. 'Seal in the shower!' Mandy smiled. 'And she loves it!'

But all good things had to end. It was soon time for Selkie's feed. So Mandy left Ross to turn off the shower and barricade the seal pup in the bath. When she came back with the fish, she looked puzzled. 'Where's Iona?' Mandy asked. 'I can't find her anywhere.'

Ross didn't look up from fixing the chairs in

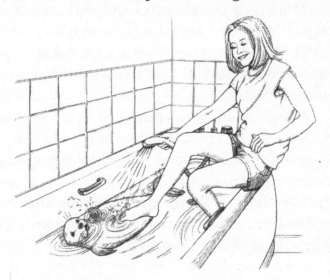

position so that Selkie couldn't escape. 'Gone home.'

Mandy frowned. 'What do you mean, gone home?'

'Back to the sea. I took her down to the beach this afternoon to see if she was ready.' Ross had put on his offhand tone of voice, but by now Mandy could recognise it as a sign that he was covering up his true feelings. 'She practically galloped into the water. She was off like a shot,' he told her. 'She headed out across the bay without even looking back.'

Mandy listened quietly. She pictured gentle Iona leaving the shore far behind, and she sighed. 'I know I ought to be glad, but . . .'

'I know,' Ross agreed. He took a last, lingering look at Selkie. 'Will you give her her supper?' he asked.

Without waiting for an answer, he left Mandy to feed the fish to the hungry pup.

She guessed what he was thinking; today Iona, tomorrow or the day after, it would be Selkie's turn. However glad you were that an animal had got better and was fit to go back to the wild, it always hurt to say goodbye.

Six

'Why not take Selkie to the beach today?' Mary McLeod asked Mandy next morning. 'It's time that pup got the scent of seawater in her nostrils again!' She was setting off for work with Mandy's mum. Adam Hope had decided to stay at home and spend the day in the sun once more. He was sitting reading in a deckchair on the lawn.

Mandy stood at the door eating an apple. Selkie sat at her feet like a faithful puppy-dog, staring up at her with big, dark eyes. 'OK,' she promised. 'It won't be too hard to get her down there. She follows me everywhere I go!'

Her dad peered over the top of his book. 'Mandy had a little seal,' he chanted, 'Its fur was white as snow; And everywhere that Mandy went . . . !'

She tutted. 'Selkie's fur isn't white any more, Dad. That was her baby fur! She's grown up now, aren't you, Selkie?' Mandy bent to stroke her soft grey coat.

'See if she wants a swim.' Emily Hope suggested, as she squeezed by and headed for the car. 'And remember; don't get too attached to her.' She knew Mandy of old.

'Too late, I suspect.' Adam Hope watched Selkie flop across the lawn close on Many's heels.

Mandy waved goodbye to her mum and Mary. 'It's not me; it's Selkie!' Mandy protested. 'I can't help it if she follows me!'

'She probably thinks you're her mum,' Mr Hope pointed out. 'When you think about it, you're the nearest thing she's got to one.' He teased Mandy by barking and flapping his arms together like a seal.

Mandy pretended to ignore him. She tossed her head and headed for a home-made rope-swing slung over the bough of an oak-tree in the far corner of the garden. While she sat on

it and swung to and fro, Selkie settled down
for a sunbathe.

The morning drifted on. The sun rose and
grew hot. There was scarcely a breeze to rustle
the leaves or keep them cool as it reached its
height. Two fallow deer ventured down from
Castle Wood to graze on the edge of the lawn.
Selkie snoozed on, while Mandy watched the
deer.

She could have let the moment last for ever;
blue sky, hot sun, the graceful animals advanc-
ing without fear. But her dad woke with a start
from his own midday snooze. The startled deer
sprang for the cover of the trees. Selkie raised
her head to look for Mandy. She panted in the
heat.

'OK, come on.' Mandy jumped off the swing
and went to the edge of the wood to wait for
Selkie. 'Let's go to the beach!' There was no
more putting it off. It was time to show Selkie
the sea.

'Do you want me to come?' her dad said.

'No thanks.' She smiled at him. 'If it's time
for her to go, I'd rather do it by myself.'

He nodded. 'I'll see you later, then. I'm here
all afternoon if you want me.'

'Thanks, Dad.'

Mandy set off slowly. Selkie followed, eager but clumsy on land. She bobbed up and down, head swaying, blundering through the undergrowth. At Kilmarten Castle they stopped for a rest. It was there that Selkie smelled the sea. A breeze had picked up and came in across the bay, skimming the top of Castle Hill. Salt was in the air; the smell of the waves. Selkie's head went up. She looked at Mandy, eager to be on their way.

Mandy gazed down at her and nodded. 'OK, I'm coming.' They went quickly down the hill, walked clear of the trees on to the wide stretch of smooth white pebbles. Selkie saw the sea, raised her head and gave a loud, pleased bark. Then the seal pup rushed for the gently rolling waves, the lapping water and the clear green depths.

'What happened next?' Ross met Mandy in the castle clearing. She was on her way home from the beach and she was dripping wet. He'd run down from the tower as soon as he'd spotted her.

'Selkie dived straight in,' Mandy said. 'Just

like you said with Iona. But she didn't swim off; oh no! She just pottered around in the shallow water.'

'So then what did you do?' Ross had spent all morning in the castle ruins, as he did when he wanted to be by himself. He hadn't realised Mandy had taken Selkie to the shore until he'd spotted her dripping figure coming back through the clearing. Her blonde hair was stuck to her cheeks, and her T-shirt and shorts were wringing wet. Her trainers squelched as she walked.

'I tried talking nicely to her,' Mandy explained. 'I told her how wonderful life at sea would be. Millions of fish, sunny rocks to stretch out on, no one to bother her.'

The corners of Ross's mouth began to twitch. 'Did she believe you?'

'No, she didn't listen to a word I said. She just splashed about and waited for me to go in the water with her. She wanted to play.' Mandy flopped on to the grass and took off her shoes. She tipped the seawater out on to the ground, then wrung out the hem of her T-shirt.

'So you did?' Ross found it funny that Mandy had gone swimming fully-dressed.

'I had to show her what to do, didn't I? She had to get the idea that seals belong in the sea!' It was a fact that the playful pup seemed to have forgotten. When Mandy had joined her in the water, Selkie had come to twist and roll, to tumble over her and dive underneath.

'How long did it take?'

'Ages.' They'd swum close to the shore. Selkie had loved every minute. But each time Mandy had tried to head back to dry land, the pup had followed. 'In the end I had to sneak away when she wasn't looking.' She'd waited until Selkie was nosing through some eelgrass near a rocky island, then she'd made for the beach. She ran for it, hoping to reach Castle Wood before Selkie came up for air.

'Do you think she'll be OK?' Mandy asked Ross now. She'd dashed off without looking back. It wasn't the kind of goodbye she would have chosen. She felt worried and guilty, as if she'd let Selkie down.

Ross was still grinning. 'Ask her yourself!' He listened to a rustling through the undergrowth, then pointed to the path which Mandy had used. 'Here she comes right now!'

There was a short bark, then a lolloping

shape appeared. Selkie wriggled out of the bushes and flopped across the grass, making a beeline for Mandy. Too surprised to move, Mandy felt a whiskery face snuffle up to her as the pup threw herself against her.

'Oh!' Mandy was speechless. She hugged the seal, who was covered in twigs and leaves after her dash through the wood.

'It looks like she doesn't fancy life at sea just yet.' Ross wasn't surprised. 'She prefers bed and breakfast as Kilmarten Lodge!'

Selkie lived on in the lap of luxury through Saturday, Sunday and Monday. She lay on a towel in the bathroom, gobbling up herring and having her back scratched by Mandy. She wallowed in the bath or followed her 'stepmother' round the house, from kitchen to lounge, and from garden swing to the tower at Kilmarten Castle. Everywhere she went, she sniffed and poked around with her blunt nose, curious as a kitten.

Mandy's favourite time of all was in the evening, sitting with Selkie in the late sun, when even the pup had run out of energy. Then they would laze in the garden. Selkie would stretch her rubbery body out long and thin, raise her head, bob and wave her neck through the air, while Mandy fed her scraps of fish.

'Tomorrow,' she would sigh, when Mary McLeod reminded her that it was nearly time for Selkie to leave them.

'And tomorrow, and tomorrow!' her dad teased. It was Monday evening, and they all sat round a table by the french windows, watching Mandy play with the seal.

'I am trying, honestly!' She waggled a piece of fish just out of Selkie's reach. She stretched and nipped it clean out of her hand. 'She comes down to the beach with us every day now, doesn't she, Ross?'

He nodded. 'But she just swims round for a bit, then comes back to the shore.'

'But she caught a fish today.' Mandy was keen to show that they were making progress. 'All by herself.'

'That's good.' Her mum lifted her wine glass. 'I'll drink to that!'

The conversation drifted on. Mary told Mandy that her guillemot was almost better after four days of round-the-clock care from Andrew. 'But the coastguards are still keeping an eye on the oil slick that caused the problem. The tide keeps on bringing it too close to the shore for comfort,' she reported. 'So far it hasn't done too much damage.'

Mandy was relieved to hear that the guillemot had recovered. 'I'll tell Gordon tomorrow morning.' The fisherman would be pleased that their rescue work had paid off.

Ross looked at his watch. 'We could go now if you like. It's high tide.' Gordon would be bringing in his evening catch about now.

It was a perfect evening as Mandy, Ross and Selkie set off for the beach. They followed the usual path through the wood, past Kilmarten Castle and down the hill to the sea. Selkie poked around and took her time as usual. There were scents to follow, moths to chase. But when the seal pup got wind of the sea, she was off. Her tubby body practically tumbled over itself to get into the water.

'Hi, Gordon!' Mandy waved at the old man as he hauled his boat on to the beach. They'd timed it exactly right.

The fisherman growled hello and stopped for a chat. There were scraps for Selkie, and for the five or six seals who had followed the boat across the bay. They bobbed in the water at a safe distance, then leaped high for the tiddlers that Gordon threw.

'Our guillemot's nearly better,' Mandy told him. 'He's all cleaned up. He didn't swallow the oil, so it didn't actually poison him.'

Gordon grunted his satisfaction. 'Well done.' He gathered his catch from the boat, ready to plot off home.

Ross offered to tip the empty boat on to its side. 'We'll do this for you!' He got busy, while Gordon thanked them and set off. Meanwhile, Selkie slipped into the water to play. When Mandy and Ross had finished turning the boat upside down, they looked up and were surprised to see one of the wild seals swimming close to the shore, while the others still circled at a distance. Selkie saw him too, and stayed quietly where she was.

'That's Misty,' Ross whispered as the stranger approached. He was a young male, swimming slowly, with only his head breaking the surface. He came up to Selkie and circled round her; once, twice, three times. 'Watch this!'

Selkie turned on the spot. Her eyes followed her young admirer. Then Misty swam off a few metres out to sea. Selkie followed. She seemed to test whether or not to venture further.

'Look, she's changed her mind!' Mandy saw the pup swim back towards the shore where they stood. They waited and watched.

Selkie swam in smaller and smaller circles. Her dark eyes darted from Ross and Mandy to her new friend. Misty waited patiently. Beyond him, the older seals swam and dived.

Mandy crouched at the water's edge. 'Go on!' she whispered softly. 'Misty wants to be your friend. He's waiting for you. It's time to go!'

Selkie made one last circle through the shallow waves. The wild seal called for her to come. Selkie dipped her head below the surface, turned and swam away for good.

Seven

Without Selkie, the lodge felt empty. Mandy had too much time on her hands, and a feeling that the holiday was coming to an end. Soon they would have to leave Jura and the beautiful seals behind. She turned her thoughts to Welford and Animal Ark, and her friends at home. What had James Hunter been getting up to without her, she wondered. Had he got the postcard she'd sent?

'A penny for them?' Emily Hope sat quietly at the breakfast table next morning.

Mandy sat opposite, chin in hands, elbows on the table. Her dad was out with Ross, hoping to see the otter that had dammed the stream half a kilometre inland from the lodge. Mary had already set off for work. 'My thoughts aren't worth even a penny,' she sighed. Today she hadn't even wanted to go exploring for otters with Ross and her dad.

'Cheer up. Just think of Selkie with her little colony out there in that perfect bay.' Her mum knew how Mandy was feeling. 'You know you've done well this holiday?'

She nodded. 'Thanks, Mum.' There was no point moping, so she stood up and began to clear the table. 'Do you fancy trying to find out where Ross and Dad have got to?'

'Good idea.'

'I've never seen an otter.'

'No, they're becoming very rare.' Emily Hope told her that their woodland habitat had been cut back until only a few survived. Mandy got ready, suddenly keen to make the most of the day.

'Cagouls on, I think.' Emily Hope looked out of the window at a bank of clouds gathering over Castle Wood. 'And wellies. It looks like rain.'

They set off soon after nine to catch up with

the others, down a track that led away from the coast; two brightly dressed figures under a gloomy sky. Emily Hope wore a purple waterproof jacket, zipped to the chin. Mandy's was a royal blue.

'Funnily enough, I don't think it's going to rain after all.' Mandy's mum kept an eye on the weather as they met the stream and began to follow it further inland. Clouds hung heavy over the island, but the air was warm and still. 'Not yet, at least.'

Mandy had her mind on other things. 'There's Dad!' She saw him standing astride the stream, peering into the fast-running water. 'It looks like they've found the dam.'

She ran ahead, eager to see the otter. To either side of the stream there were thick hazel bushes growing between mossy boulders, and steep banks covered in ferns.

'Don't tread in the water!' Ross warned. He was perched on a high rock behind one of the bushes. 'You'll scare him off.'

'Have you seen him yet?' She scrambled up the rock for a better view.

'No, but here's his dam.' Mr Hope pointed to a strong barrier built across the stream. It was made of branches and twigs, wedged between rocks. Above the dam was a deep, clear pool; below it, the water trickled on its course down the hill. 'Amazing engineers, aren't they?' He pointed out how the otter had chosen the ideal place to dam the stream in order to trap small fish in the pool he'd created.

'What now?' Mandy longed to see the creature himself.

'Now we wait,' Ross said quietly.

Mandy's mum and dad chose out of the way places on the opposite bank. They crouched out of sight, hiding behind boulders and ferns. If they all kept quite still and were very patient, they might be in luck.

Mandy's legs grew stiff and began to ache. They'd been waiting for over an hour, watching all kinds of wildlife visit the stream. Tiny voles crept through the ferns, dainty dippers visited the water's edge and pecked at insects. Then, just when they were losing hope, the master-builder himself appeared.

The otter swam out of his hiding-place just a few metres upstream. His head was broad and flat, his ears tiny, his eyes bright. He came stealthily, only his flat head showing, swimming this way and that. There was scarcely a ripple in the smooth pond as he paddled silently with his webbed feet.

They held their breath. This was a rare and wonderful sight. Mandy hoped he would show himself properly, and, sure enough, he clambered out of the water on his squat legs, trailing his thick, smooth tail. He climbed slowly across his dam, as clumsy on land as he was swift and graceful in the water. He was the size of a small terrier, with a fat face, sharp teeth and coarse brown fur. Mandy loved his strange waddling walk and split-second dive back into the pool.

Seconds later he came to the surface, a tiny silver fish gripped between his jaws. Then he swam upstream, going against the strong current, holding his catch firmly in his sharp teeth, until eventually his silent shape vanished amongst the weeds and rocks of a far-off bank.

'Amazing!' Mandy whispered to Ross.

Across the stream her dad stood up to ease his stiff back. He glanced up at the sky. 'I don't know about you lot, but I don't like the look of those clouds.'

They decided it would be best to head for

home. Even Mandy admitted it would be no fun waiting in a downpour for the otter to return.

'Was that thunder?' Emily Hope listened carefully.

Mandy looked at the sky. The clouds had turned purple and black, rolling in from the sea.

Only Ross seemed unconcerned. He set off walking, flicking a long stick against his leg, determined to ignore the heavy, cold drops of rain that had begun to fall.

'Uh-oh!' Mandy broke into a trot. 'Here it comes!' The raindrops spattered the dusty track with dark splashes. They fell faster, with a great roar of thunder. Soon the rain came down in a torrent.

Hoods up, heads down, they ran for shelter. A wind got up over the sea and drove the rain into their faces. Lightning forked through the black sky, thunder crashed.

'I'm soaked through!' Mandy's dad gasped as they dashed for the house. His beard dripped, the rain lashed against him, the wind tore the hood from his head. 'Quickly, everyone, get inside!' He held the door open while Mandy, Mrs Hope and Ross stumbled into the house.

'Phew!' Emily Hope unzipped her jacket in the safety of the kitchen. Outside, the lightning flashed, the thunder rolled over the island. The rain was a solid sheet of hissing water. 'If this is a summer storm, I wouldn't like to see one in winter!' She went to put the kettle on to make tea.

'There's the phone!' Above the rattle of thunder, Mandy heard it ring. 'I'll go!' She kicked off her wellingtons and raced to answer it.

It was Mary, phoning from the rescue centre. 'Hello, Mandy, is everyone all right over there? Listen, I thought I'd better warn you not to expect me back home tonight.'

'Because of the storm?' She pictured Mary trying to drive over the mountains in torrential rain.

'Yes. What's it like where you are?'

'Pretty bad.'

'Here too. The wind has changed direction. It's blowing in from the north-east.'

Outside in the yard, a door banged. The thunder rattled the panes of the french windows.

Mary sounded worried. 'Listen, Mandy, tell Ross and your parents not to leave the house until it's passed over, OK? Tell them I have to stay here on stand-by.'

'But you can't go out on patrol in this, can you?'

'No. All we can do is wait for casualties.'

Mandy thought of Selkie on her first full day at sea. 'What kind of casualities?'

There was a pause, then Mary told her the worst. 'Oil slick victims, I'm afraid. Since the wind altered, it's bringing the slick down the strait.' She explained that the threat that had been lurking out at sea had changed course. 'It's blowing straight towards the east coast of Jura, for the islands and seal colonies of Selkie Bay. We're on emergency stand-by for the next twenty-four hours. That's the main reason I can't get home tonight.'

Mandy's heart thudded, then almost stopped.

'Mandy?' Mary sounded faint, a long way off. 'Are you OK?'

'Yes. I'll tell the others.' She gripped the phone until her knuckles turned white.

'And try not to worry too much. We're only

on stand-by. There won't be a full-scale emergency as long as the slick steers clear of the rocks.'

'I'll explain,' Mandy assured her. She put the phone down, and felt her legs wobble as she walked slowly into the kitchen.

They knew straight away that something was wrong. Ross was the first to look round when she came in, but he stared in silence.

'Come and sit down.' Mandy's mum pulled out a chair. 'What's wrong? Have you had a shock of some sort?' She handed her a mug of piping hot tea.

Mandy tried to shape a sensible warning sentence. She gazed blankly at the window as the storm raged on. The wind had whipped the clouds into a menacing, racing mass.

'It's the oil slick,' Ross cut in, his voice hard-edged and certain. 'It's heading this way, isn't it?'

She nodded. 'Unless the wind turns again and blows it out to sea. It could even hit us right here at Selkie Bay!'

Ross nodded. His mouth set in a grim line, then he turned and walked out, slamming the door as he went.

* * *

The storm raged through the middle of the day. It drenched the island in cold rain, and it tore through the trees and across the mountain tops. Mandy watched helplessly through the blurred windows. She heard the rush of gale force winds sweep by the lodge. Then, at three o'clock, the rain stopped as suddenly as it had started. The clouds parted and the thunder rolled off into the distance. Overhead, the sky was blue.

'Thank heavens for that.' Adam Hope looked up from his crossword.

Mandy too heaved a sigh of relief. She went through the house looking for Ross. There was no sign of him.

'I just saw him cutting through the garden towards the castle,' Emily Hope told her. She knew Mandy well enough to guess what she would do next. 'If you're thinking of following him, put your cagoul on. It's still pretty windy out there.'

'And take care,' her dad instructed. 'The storm might have done some damage to the woods. Watch out for fallen trees.'

'I won't be long,' Mandy promised. She

wanted to check with Ross what would happen to the oil slick now that the storm was over. She zipped her jacket and set off through the sodden grass, pushing aside dripping undergrowth as she headed for Kilmarten Castle.

But when she got there, she found that the ruin was empty. Mandy stepped inside the crumbling walls and went upstairs on to the balcony. She stood at the door and called up the dark tower. Dry wings flitted, an owl hooted, but there was no answer from Ross. She checked once more. Either he was hiding from her, or else he'd headed on towards the beach. She decided to follow the path through the woods to Selkie Bay.

That was where she found him, out on the headland, staring across to the curved coastline where the seals had their haul-outs. The wind blew so fiercely that it almost swept Mandy off her feet as she struggled out to join him.

Without turning round, Ross seemed to know that she'd arrived. 'I came to look for Selkie,' he told her. 'I thought she might have swum back for shelter.'

Mandy scanned the rough, grey waves. The

storm had churned up eelgrass and sea-kelp, and disturbed the sandy seabed. But there was no sign of a friendly, familiar head bobbing towards them. Further off, across the sky, the rocky haul-outs were deserted. 'She didn't,' Mandy said emptily.

'I thought she might have,' he insisted. 'Sometimes they swim for the shore if you've only just released them into the sea. It's safer.'

Mandy frowned. The wind tugged and tore at her. 'Isn't she safe where she is now?' The lightning, thunder and rain had blown away. Surely the worst was over.

Ross didn't answer straight away. 'The problem is, she probably swam out to sea with the others instead. That's what the adults do if there's a storm. They head away from the rocks.' He looked for signs of life, still hoping to see Selkie sheltering somewhere in the bay.

'Why is that a problem?' Mandy didn't see what Ross was getting at. Why was he still so worried?

He turned to face her at last. 'Because, right now that's where the oil slick is. Beyond the bay, somewhere just off this coast.'

She looked up at the clear sky. The wind was still strong and fierce.

'And the tide's turning,' he went on. 'It's starting to come in again. And with the wind still in the wrong direction, the oil is going to hit us head on. I know it is!'

But Mandy said he couldn't know for sure. 'The wind is still strong, but it could die down at any moment. The slick could slide down the strait past Selkie Bay, and never hit the coast at all. Let's hope for the best,' she pleaded.

He nodded, but his eyes showed that he didn't agree. 'Anyway, come on,' he said abruptly. 'There's no point hanging around here. Selkie didn't come back, so there's nothing we can do about it.'

They turned and went with the wind behind them. It almost swept them along the headland back on to the beach. The wind and sun had already dried the pebbles, and Mandy took off her cagoul and tied the arms round her waist, letting it flap behind her. She followed Ross up the hill towards the castle.

Then, as they came into the clearing, the wind gave its final warning. It swirled up from behind them, carrying salt air off the sea. It swept across the open space as they clung to tree branches to stay on their feet. The gust battered the castle walls, rushed at the ancient door. Hinges creaked, and the door swung open with a crash.

Mandy and Ross saw a flurry of dead leaves rise from the corners of the central hall. The brown leaves rose and whirled in a spiral. Wind clattered at the rusting spears and shields, and brought them crashing on to the stairs. It forced its way up through rotten ceilings, tunnelled down corridors, flew up again through great holes in the roof. Everywhere it reached, it brought destruction. Doors were wrenched open and off their hinges. Wood splintered. Plaster crumbled and fell.

Mandy held her hands to her ears. Ross looked on in dismay. The laird's house was being torn apart by the wind which rushed through the empty rooms, around the sides of the tall, grey tower, and on towards the mountains of Jura, bringing another disaster fast on its heels.

Eight

'There must be something we can do!' Adam Hope had listened to Ross's description of the wildlife tragedy that was about to hit Selkie Bay. He paced the floor of the kitchen, feeling helpless.

'Well, we can't turn the tide, that's for sure.' Emily Hope spoke more calmly. She turned to Ross. 'Couldn't the coastguards go up in their helicopter and spray dispersant on to the oil before it reaches the shore?'

Mandy knew that pouring special chemicals on to the sea could help to break up the slick.

Ross thought about it. He pushed his hair

back from his forehead, fidgeted on his chair, then got up to pace the floor with Mandy's dad. 'They might be able to,' he admitted.

Mandy wanted to spring into action. 'Let's ring them then and get them to do it before it's too late!'

Ross shook his head. 'No. For one thing, a helicopter can't go up in this wind.'

No one argued with this. Ross would know it only too well, for this was how his own father had died, in a rescue helicopter during a storm.

'But if the wind were to drop, could they be ready?' Emily Hope thought it might still be worth a try.

'Yes, but the second thing is that even if the wind did drop, they wouldn't want to spray dispersant this close to the shore.' He was tense, constantly looking out of the window, as if he felt trapped inside the lodge.

'Why not?' Mandy tried to follow the reasons. Surely doing *something* to clear up the oil was better than doing nothing.

'Because sometimes the dispersant does as much damage to the wildlife as the oil itself,' Ross said. He had already thought all this through. 'They have to use strong chemicals to get rid of the oil, and they can kill the small sea organisms that the fish feed on. Or else the chemicals get in through the fish's skin, then the gulls and the seals eat the fish, and so on.'

Mandy sighed. 'So it's hopeless, then?'

'What about putting a boom across the bay to keep the oil out?' Mr Hope raked his memory for all the ways he knew of saving wildlife. 'A kind of floating barrier to stop the slick.'

'Too expensive?' Mrs Hope guessed. She looked to Ross for an answer.

He nodded. 'And too late.' Minutes were ticking by while they sat doing nothing.

'If only the wind would die down.' Mandy stood by the window. She could see the tops of the trees bending under the force of the gale, hear it whooshing through the leafy branches.

Suddenly the phone rang. Mandy's dad was nearest to it, so he picked up the receiver. 'It's Mary,' he told them. Then he listened intently, nodding and saying, yes, they would come across straight away. When he put the phone down, he explained the new plan.

'Mary wants Emily and me to drive over to the rescue centre,' he told Mandy and Ross.

'They've brought in several seabirds which have been washed up after the storm. Most of them are covered in oil, and they need two extra pairs of hands. I said we'd help.'

'Any seals?' Mandy asked, her heart giving a lurch.

'Not so far. Mary wants you two to stay here to keep an eye on things. We need you to keep a lookout on this east coast, to give us an early warning if and when the oil slick hits the shore. Will you do that?'

They both nodded, though Mandy was torn between wanting to help at the rescue centre and acting as lookout here. There were sick birds actually needing help, yet over here there were hundreds more still in danger.

Her parents rushed to get ready. They put on warm sweaters and took anything else they thought they might need out to the Land-rover. Mandy and Ross watched quietly from the door.

'Remember; phone the centre the minute you get any definite news of the slick,' Mr Hope said. He slung his vets' bag into the vehicle. 'Perhaps Gordon McRae will know what's happening. Give him a ring and say we're all on tenterhooks, wanting to know exactly where it is.'

Emily Hope was half in the Land-rover, hanging on to the door frame. There wasn't a second to lose. 'And don't do anything foolish!' she warned. 'No heroics. Put your own safety first, whatever you do!'

Again they promised.

'It's us against the wind and the tide,' Mrs Hope reminded them. 'And we're only puny little human beings. I don't want you to do anything dangerous, OK?'

'Don't worry, we can look after ourselves!' Mandy urged them on their way. They watched the Land-rover drive out of the yard and take the inland road. Red tail-lights winked, she waved, then they were gone.

'I can't just stay here!' Ross stared at the telephone as if he hated it. 'What's the point of waiting for it to ring?'

'We're part of a warning system,' Mandy told him. 'Someone might try to ring us with news.'

'But we can't even see the sea from here! How can we keep a lookout if we can't see what we're looking for? Anyway, they didn't actually tell us not to leave the house, did they?'

Mandy admitted this. 'Maybe we could just go down to the shore every now and then to take a quick look. We could leave the answering machine on in case anyone wants to leave a message. And we could keep on popping back.' If Ross was out and about, no way did she want to be stuck here in the house. 'What time is it now?'

'Three forty-five. It's high tide in two hours.' The most dangerous time, when the oil slick would slide closest to the coast.

There was still no sign of the wind dying down. 'OK!' Mandy made her decision. Before the word was out of her mouth, Ross had made for the door. 'Wait for me!' She pressed the Record button on the phone and followed him.

They raced together up Castle Hill and through the clearing, fighting the wind as they came to the crest of the hill. They faced its full force on the downward path to the shore. It seemed stronger than ever, blowing straight off the sea. But as yet the bay was clear. There was no dark oil stain on its choppy surface; only sparkling silver light reflected from the sun shining down from a blue sky.

Mandy was taken aback. Everything looked normal. True, the high wind brought the waves crashing on to the shore instead of gently lapping at the pebbles. The breakers rolled into deep troughs, rose and broke with a thundering roar and a rush of white foam. But further out to sea the horizon was clear, and on the far, curving headland, she could even see the seals. They had returned to their haul-outs after the storm. 'Look, Ross!' She pointed them out.

'I know, I saw them.' He scanned the horizon, one hand shading his eyes from the bright sun. He showed Mandy the wisps of fresh cloud far out to see. 'There'll be more rain soon,' he said.

'But the clouds are tiny!' she protested. Everywhere sunlight danced on the water.

'Even so.' Ross's face was stubborn, serious. 'And look, Gordon's coming back early.' He pointed to a speck on the horizon, long before Mandy could make out what it was. 'That shows there's definitely something wrong out there!'

They waited. Slowly the little white boat rocked across the bay. It fought the waves, and steered for the shore. 'Yes, I wonder why he's back so soon?' Mandy thought aloud.

Gordon rowed steadily to within shouting distance. When he saw them, he rested his oars. 'Oil slick!' he yelled. 'I sailed straight into the middle of it, and had to turn back!'

Mandy drew a sharp breath. She ran out on to the nearby headland to shout back. She cupped both hands to her mouth. 'Which way is it heading?' she cried.

'Due east. It's coming for the bay, about half a mile out to sea!' Gordon began to row once more. He looked weary and disappointed.

Mandy ran back to help Ross haul the fishing-boat on to the beach. Gordon's nets were practically empty, and his lined face was creased into a deep frown. All along the sides of his boat there were ugly globs of oil clinging to the shiny white paint.

'See!' He gave the boat a disgusted glance. 'I thought I'd better come back to warn you. It looks to me like the oil will hit the headland opposite.'

'Where the seals are?' Mandy grasped what he was telling them. The way the wind and tide were carrying it, Gordon judged that the oil slick would crash into the haul-outs.

'Aye. Your mother will have her work cut out

this evening,' Gordon told Ross. 'Will you ring her, or do you want me to do it?'

'Would you?' Ross replied swiftly. 'Tell her where the slick is now. They'll be able to work out exactly when it'll hit the land.'

'Och, I can tell you that myself.' The old man was shrewd. He knew the tides and currents better than anyone. 'I'd say you have a hour to go before the slick reaches the bay.'

'Is that all?' Mandy felt the panic rise.

'An hour, maybe less,' he repeated. He decided to leave his boat and fishing-tackle on the beach, intent on passing on the news as soon as possible. 'I'll ring the rescue centre straight away, and tell them to expect trouble. There's that colony of seals to look out for. I don't expect they have a clue what's in store for them.' He went on up the slope, shaking his head at the terrible turn of events.

Mandy stared at Ross. In one hour or less, Selkie Bay would be plunged into a full-scale emergency. There would be no more hoping for the best, no more kidding themselves that the oil slick might slide harmlessly by. Now it was definite; their colony of seals lay directly in its path.

'I knew it,' Ross said bleakly.

Mandy saw that he was on the point of giving in. His mouth was shut tight, and he'd muttered the words through clenched teeth.

'We're not going to stand by and let this happen!' She flared up, willing him to keep on fighting. 'Come on, Ross! Selkie's out there on those rocks. And Iona and Misty and all the rest!'

'You heard what Gordon said.' Ross sounded as grim as he looked. 'This is the way it always happens. People *talk* about protecting wildlife and caring. But they don't act. They only come along when it's too late, to take photos of the mess and stick them in the papers!'

'I know. That's why *we* can't stand by and let it happen. We have to try and save the seals!'

'How?' He turned his gaze on her.

Mandy looked round. Her desperate eyes rested on Gordon's boat. He'd left it was it was, with his nets inside, two life-jackets slung in the bottom beside the small pile of herrings he'd caught before he was forced to turn back. 'Come on!' She cried, running to the boat. She stumbled in her hurry. 'You'll have to row, Ross. I'm not good enough to do it alone!' She seized the tow-rope and began to tug the boat back into the water. 'Grab the oars, give me a hand!'

'What for?' In spite of his question, Ross did run to help. They struggled into the life-jackets, then splashed into the waves. They held steady against the pounding of small pebbles and foam.

'We're going out there.' She made him jump in. 'How long will it take us to reach the far side of the bay? Fifteen minutes?'

'More like twenty.' He knew the wind and tide would hold them up.

Mandy felt the boat rock as the water swirled

round her legs. She pushed the boat further out. 'Grab the oars. You're not scared, are you?'

Without bothering to answer, Ross seized the oars and waited for her to jump in. Then he began to row.

'Head for the haul-outs,' she told him. 'We've got fish, and we know the seals are out there. What we have to do is tempt them away from the rocks where the oil is going to land!'

'You make it sound dead easy.' Their little boat already tossed in the waves, but Ross ploughed through them. He grunted as he rowed, cutting across the bay.

'No, but if Gordon could make it, so can we.' Mandy was determined to try her idea. She prayed now that Selkie was with the colony on the haul-outs, for Selkie was the one who knew her best. Maybe the seal would trust Mandy and sense that she'd come to help.

Slowly they drew near. They could tell by the pull of the current that the tide was still coming in, and with it came the wispy white clouds, building now to a dark grey bank, darkening the waves beneath them. On the rocks, the seals barked and called to the circling gulls.

'They've seen us!' Mandy warned Ross to

slow down when they came to within about two hundred metres of the haul-outs. The smooth grey rocks sloped down to the rough water. She could smell seaweed, and saw the seals shift restlessly up the slopes away from the boat. 'I think I can see Iona,' Mandy whispered. Rocked by the waves, clinging to the sides of the boat, she peered beyond the white spray.

A big, pale-grey female slid to the water's edge. She raised her head to bark at them.

'Yes, she's recognised us!' Mandy grew excited.

Ross sat with his back to the seals, rowing more slowly now. But Mandy could see over his shoulder, and that was definitely Iona coming towards them. Now, where was Selkie? Would she come when Mandy called?

'Try the fish,' Ross said. He was exhausted from rowing against the wind and tide. He slumped forward across his oars.

So Mandy reached for a herring from Gordon's catch. She took up the slippery fish and held it out for the seals to see. 'Come and get it!' she urged, calling above the sound of the waves. She knew they had to lure them away from the haul-outs before high tide; they had only half an hour to save the seals.

Iona's eagle eye was the first to spot food. Without a second thought she dived into the sea. Seconds later, her head appeared beside the boat. She barked for the fish. Mandy popped it straight into her mouth.

'Try again!' Ross struggled to keep the boat steady. They were drifting too near to the rocks, pushed by the tide. He glanced anxiously out to sea.

Tottering and swaying with the boat, Mandy managed to stand up and keep her balance. She held out another fish. Two more seals plopped eagerly into the water. That left four on the rocks; two mothers and two young ones, but none Mandy recognised. 'Come on, Selkie, where are you?' she called.

The two adventurous seals surfaced and begged for fish. They twisted and turned about the boat, circling it greedily. Then the four on the rock came to join them, followed by a powerful bull seal who appeared from behind a boulder.

'That's Shadow,' Ross said. He gazed at the empty haul-outs. 'It doesn't look like Selkie and Misty are here.'

But as he spoke, two more lithe shapes came from behind the rock. They barked and tumbled, rolled down the slopes and flipped into the water, fresh from the game they'd been playing.

Mandy's eyes lit up. It was the two pups; Mandy would have known them anywhere. 'Here they come!' She'd kept back a big, juicy fish. Now she held it up for Selkie. 'Here you are, girl, this is for you!'

The boat lurched, but Mandy stayed on her feet. Misty followed Selkie to join the other seals around the boat. Now the whole colony was clear of the rocks. All Mandy and Ross had to do was to tempt them away, closer to the shore, away from the poisonous oil.

Nine

Selkie jumped clean out of the water to claim her fish. Mandy was overjoyed to see her. Her seal pup had survived her first day in the sea, and her first storm. She was strong and supple, and could dive and swim with amazing speed. Best of all, she had been accepted into the Selkie Bay colony without any trouble and made herself at home.

Ross freed one hand from the oars and flung Misty a fish too. The pup caught it with a sharp snap of his strong jaws. 'OK,' he said to Mandy, 'what's the plan now?' He seemed ready to do whatever she suggested.

She looked carefully all around the bay. 'We need to draw them over towards the calmer water by Chapel Rock.' She pointed to a sheltered spot behind a scattering of smaller islands. The biggest one of these was the pyramid rock with the old chapel and the stone cross. Here, the waves broke on the near side of the rocks, then eased round them into a small inlet. The inlet was protected from the wind and the full swell of high tide. 'I'll try to get Selkie to follow us, then hopefully the others will come too.'

Ross turned the boat round with an expert paddling of the oars. But his doubts had crept in again. Since taking up Mandy's challenge, he'd rowed for all he was worth, and done exactly as she'd asked. Now, though, he spoke up. 'There's one problem.'

'What?' They still had some fish in the boat to tempt the seals with. Selkie was pleased to see them and ready to follow wherever they led. Mandy felt hopeful that her plan would succeed.

'There's going to be another storm.' As Ross glanced up at the clouds, heavy raindrops began to fall.

To Mandy this only meant that they should row faster. They had to reach the shelter of the natural harbour. 'Let's go! Do you want me to take a turn at rowing?' She offered to change places and let Ross lure the seals with the fish.

'No, you don't understand.' He tilted his head back and let the rain cool his hot face. 'If there's more thunder and lightning, the seals won't follow us to the shore.'

'Why not?' She stretched out to stroke Selkie's soft nose. The pup swam close to the coat, giving yelps of pleasure.

'Because a seal always heads out to sea during a storm. It's instinct. That's what they do.'

Mandy's hopes came crashing down. 'Are you sure?' Ross sounded so certain, but he could be wrong. '*Always*?'

He sat resting the oars, listening for the first crack of thunder that would send the seals plunging into the depths and heading for the mouth of the bay. 'I don't see how we can get them to break the habit,' he told her.

'But the oil will poison them!' Mandy couldn't believe how near they were to saving the seals, yet how far. Now, at the worst possible moment, Ross was giving her more terrible news. A fresh storm was about to break, and a slick of oil lurked there at the mouth of Selkie Bay. It was two hundred metres long, blocking the path of the seals if they did swim out to sea. Even as she stared at the horizon, Mandy fancied she saw a dark patch barring their way. Was it shadow, or was it oil? She dreaded the answer to her own question.

Just then, Selkie's head bobbed up at Ross's end of the boat. The other seals circled, waiting for fish, but Selkie took direct action. She nudged Ross's hand; there was food in the boat, so why not throw it for them to catch?

Selkie looked just like she used to when she peered over the side of the bath at them. Her eyes were huge and dark, her neck wove playfully from side to side. If she could have managed it, Selkie would have slid into the boat to grab the fish for herself.

Her sweet face prodded Ross into action of his own. He grabbed the oars and rowed off a little way. 'Oh no you don't! he warned. 'You have to follow us if you want dessert!'

Selkie barked. She was disappointed, but she swam after the boat. The other seals gathered and watched curiously.

'Good girl!' Mandy called softly. They were going to try, whatever Ross said about the storm. By now she was sure that the long, dark shadow on the sea was in fact oil. It floated in a solid mass, riding in with the tide, closer and closer. 'Come this way with us!'

Selkie hesitated. The seal pup turned to Misty and Iona, who held back amongst the group. The seals must have sensed the storm, but although the rain lashed down, as yet there was no lightning, no thunder. They were poised, ready to head for the open sea, but still interested in the fish lying in the bottom of the little boat.

Mandy willed the pup to trust her again. It wasn't just fish, but safety that she offered. 'Come on, Selkie!'

Ross eased off the oars. He let the boat drift. They were soaked to the skin, buffeted by the waves. Unless they got a move on, the oil slick would slide through the mouth of the bay and be upon them. All this would have been for nothing.

'Selkie, please!' Until twenty-four hours ago, she and the seal pup had gone everywhere

together. Please let her follow them now, Mandy prayed silently.

'Thunder!' Ross whispered. He'd heard it, faint but definite. Two seals in the group twisted in the water and dived out of sight.

But Selkie ignored the distant rumble. With her eyes fixed on Mandy, she swam to the boat.

'Oh, clever girl, she's following us!' Mandy gasped. The two diving seals came to the surface again, but not for a second would Mandy take her eyes off Selkie now. 'Start rowing, Ross. She's going to come with us!'

They bobbed and dipped through the rough sea, trailed by Selkie, then by Misty and Iona. The rest of the colony waited. Then Shadow with the wise, whiskered face made up his mind. He would follow the youngsters. Something stronger than instinct had got to work, as gradually all the seals swam towards the shore.

Mandy held her breath, Ross pulled for the shelter of the natural harbour. The dark oil slick gained on them as the tide surged in. A strong current took it against the headland, where it crashed and broke up into a black spray on the empty rocks.

Mandy felt a wrench inside her as the eerie

wave broke. There, where a few minutes earlier, the seals had basked on their haul-outs, was a deadly dark-brown froth of oil. 'Keep going,' she whispered to Ross.

He rowed out of the path of the oil, drawing the seals after him. 'We did it!' he cried as he saw the slick break up in a million drops behind them. 'We saved the seals!'

But their boat itself was in danger now, as it approached the scattered islands at the entrance to their harbour. The currents pulled them here and there, too strong for Ross to resist.

Selkie swam rapidly alongside the rocking, spinning boat, as if she knew that the rocks could easily smash it. The other seals gathered round. They overtook the boat, and tried to guide it through narrow, swift-running channels past Chapel Rock.

The rescued turned rescuers; Selkie and the seals took up the task of leading Ross and Mandy to safety.

Ten

Mandy clung tight to the sides of the boat. A wave caught them and rushed them in a surge of white water towards Chapel Rock. The seals dipped below the surface and disappeared.

'Watch out, Ross!' Mandy saw the black cliff loom ahead. Then the boat spun round. It missed the jagged rocks and swept on.

'Mandy, the oar!' Ross lurched sideways, tipping the boat, but failing to catch hold of the oar. It bounced like driftwood out of reach, and splintered on the rocks. They were out of control, and though they could see that the seals had made it through the narrow channels into the harbour, their boat still bobbed like a cork in the wild currents.

'Hold tight!' she cried again. Another wave, twice as high as the boat, huge and powerful, rolled towards them.

Ross tried to pull the second oar into the boat and grip the sides. But he wasn't quick enough. They soared high on the wave, and came sweeping down towards the rocks. He lost the oar in the swell, ducking his head as the wave broke.

It crashed around them, pouring into the boat, tossing it this way and that. Mandy clung on. She was drenched, blinded by the salt water. She felt them lurch to the side. She knew that they were about to capsize, and gave a cry as she was flung far out of the boat.

Mandy sank beneath the stormy surface among long strands of eelgrass which snaked round her legs and arms. She opened her eyes and pulled herself free, kicking away from the weeds towards clearer water. Then she swam underwater with strong, determined strokes. Her lungs began to ache and the cold seeped through to her bones, but she hoped to swim clear of danger, to follow Selkie and the seals to safety.

At last Mandy came up for air. There were rocks all around. It was hard to tell which way she'd swum. She gasped and struggled towards a rock. She knew she had to cling to it and brace herself against the force of the next huge wave.

Where was Ross? Where was their boat? Mandy was searching for a handhold, discovering that she had indeed found an underwater way through the swirling channels, when she saw the upturned boat. Its white hull bobbed in the distance in the calmer waters of the natural harbour. Three of the seals circled it as if looking for Mandy and Ross. The others waited quietly by the shore.

Another wave broke. Mandy held tight. She was more sheltered then before; the wave had lost its full force by the time it reached her. Then two heads appeared nearby, circling anxiously. Selkie and Misty had come to keep watch.

'I'm OK!' Mandy cried. She was out of danger. But there had been no sign of Ross since the boat went down. Had eelgrass wound itself round his body? Had he been knocked unconscious by the mighty waves?

Selkie launched herself towards Mandy. She came close to her and slithered on to the same rock. She seemed to wait for Mandy to follow her up the rock to safety, so slowly, painfully Mandy did what the seal wanted. Her body was bruised and battered, her lungs hurt, and the salt water stung her eyes.

Then Misty called Selkie back into the sea. Mandy's pup flipped from the rock, dived and disappeared. Misty turned and vanished round the rocky headland. Mandy almost called out in panic for them to come back.

She could hear them but not see them. They were out of sight, not far away. Too exhausted to move, she shouted. 'I'm here, Selkie. What do you want?'

Soon the pup reappeared. She swam back to Mandy's rock, climbed on to it and pulled herself still higher. Again she seemed to want Mandy to follow. From nearby, Misty called.

So Mandy dragged herself up the rough rock, aware now that it was Chapel Rock itself. She glanced up and saw the outline of the stone cross standing at its peak. The rain pelted down, and the storm clouds swirled around the bleak monument.

Selkie led the way across a seaweed-strewn mass of boulders, down again towards the water. Mandy clambered after her, feeling the lash of the wind and the waves.

Then she saw Ross. He was lying in the next inlet, his arm hooked around a sharp spear of rock, his head hanging. He was half in the water, half out. Misty kept guard close by, waiting for help to arrive.

'Ross!' Mandy slithered towards him in the rain and spray. Did she see him raise his head? Selkie took a different route and slid back into the water to wait with Misty.

Mandy crouched over Ross. His face was deathly white, his arm cut and bleeding. 'Wake up, Ross, please!' she cried. She shifted him on to the rock as best she could. He was a dead-weight and the rocks were dangerously slippery.

Slowly he opened his eyes and looked at her.

'Are you hurt?' she gasped.

'It's my leg; I can't move it.' He used his good arm to find a handhold, groping and gasping as he rolled on to his side.

'Hold on!' She hooked her arms under his

armpits and dragged him clear of the water.

Ross groaned. 'I think it's broken!' He sounded weak. His face was clenched, his head thrust back against the rock.

'Don't worry, you're safe now,' Mandy reassured him. 'Misty and Selkie found you. Listen, don't try to move any more. The water can't reach you up here.' She peered through the rain at the waves below. The seal pups were still there, round heads bobbing in the white foam. 'Anyhow, I think the tide's beginning to turn.' The current sucked away from the rocks, and the waves seemed to come in with less force.

'Where are we?' He lay back, eyes closed.

'We're on Chapel Rock. It's OK; all the seals made it!'

'What happened to Gordon's boat?'

'We capsized. Don't you remember? But I spotted it close to the shore, still in one piece.'

'And what about the oil?' Slowly things came back to him.

'It broke up on the haul-outs. But now the tide's started to go out, it'll be pulled back out to sea, what's left of it.'

'It didn't hit the shore?'

'No, just the headland. And we got the seals off just in time.' Mandy decided to try and shelter Ross from the wind. She took off her dripping cagoul and formed it into a wind-shield by anchoring each side under two heavy rocks. 'What will happen to the shellfish on the haul-outs?' She didn't expect the bay to escape all oil damage completely.

He shook his head. 'No chance. The fish spawn, the seaweed, the shellfish will all be poisoned.'

'So the seals can't go back there?'

'Not until someone's cleaned up the rocks.'

This was a problem for the future. For now they still had to look out for themselves. They might be safe from the storm at sea, but how long would it be before help arrived? The weather made it impossible for anyone to come looking for them on Chapel Rock, even if they knew where to start. Mandy remembered that no one had seen them set out across the bay before the storm broke. She recalled too her mum's orders not to do anything dangerous, and the truth of her warning that human beings were tiny and helpless against the forces of nature.

Ross groaned as he lay beside her on the rock. His body shivered from head to foot. Mandy realised she must do more to keep him warm. Like the accident victims she helped to treat at Animal Ark, she could see that he was suffering from shock. The pain in his leg must be almost unbearable.

'It's OK, the rain's easing off,' she told him. 'It'll soon stop, then they'll come to find us.' She shielded him with her cagoul. Close to the rocks, Selkie swam in and out of the inlet, waiting with them.

Ross tried to keep up a brave face, but his teeth chattered. He felt himself drift off dizzily and lose sense of where he was. He kept asking Mandy questions about the oil. She repeated the same reply: 'The seals are safe. And they saved our lives. Don't worry, everything's going to be OK.'

The rain did soon ease. The ebbing tide drew the storm clouds out to sea. Then, quite suddenly, Mandy felt the wind change direction, from the north east to a westerly that blew clear and fresh off the Atlantic. The thunder and lightning were gone, and the waves grew calm.

But it was still cold. Evening was drawing in. The light turned golden on the calm water where the seals still waited. Mandy huddled over Ross, talking to him to keep him awake. She'd wrapped her cagoul around his shivering body now, told him calmly that rescue would come soon.

Inside, she was scared. What if night fell before anyone found them? Could Ross survive a night in the open with a broken leg? She realised that he might die of exposure as his body temperature dropped. To her, it felt as if they were running out of time.

'Don't try and move!' she told him again. She'd decided to climb to the summit of the rock, to the stone cross and chapel. From there she would be able to see the whole of Selkie Bay.

'Don't worry, I won't!' Ross managed a faint smile. 'Right now I'm not going anywhere!'

'Selkie and Misty will keep an eye on you,' Mandy promised. She checked to see that the pups were still close by. Then she set off up the rocky hill, hoping against hope that there would be someone out there looking for them. Yet she knew that her mum and dad were busy at the rescue centre on the far side of Jura, and that no one would venture out fishing until they were sure that the slick had gone. Mandy expected to reach the cross and look out over an empty bay.

The wind blew hard through the tiny ruined chapel at the top of the hill. For a moment Mandy took refuge against its sheltered side. She got her breath back, but as she crouched there she recalled the story of Chapel Rock. It was from here that the people of the sea called to their dead laird in Kilmarten Castle. It was here where they trapped the souls of men who had hunted and killed them. She shivered in the shadows, as if the place were truly haunted.

Then she steeled herself to step out towards the cross on the summit. She looked out over the golden water. There, on the sheltered side of the bay, their seal colony swam amongst the shadowy rocks. She heard them call; a high, whining sound above the wind. There was the empty white shore of the bay rising to Castle Hill and the silent grey tower where the ghost of the last laird was rumoured to live. There was the long, straight headland, and there, stepping round the base of the cross, Mandy could look out to the mouth of the bay and the open sea.

Then came the distant curving headland and the ruined haul-outs of the seals. Mandy paused to look again. She couldn't see anything, but she thought she heard something. She strained to listen. Yes; there was the faint sound of a motor out by the haul-outs. And now there was a boat weaving its way around the headland, in and out of the inlets; a small, grey inflatable with three people on board!

'Over here!' Mandy waved her arms and yelled. It was the patrol boat. She recognised the low, flat shape. It was too far away for them to hear, and she couldn't see who the people were, but she knew she must attract their attention. They had to see her; they had to! 'Over here, *please*!'

Eleven

But the boat turned away into another inlet. They must be searching for seals injured by the oil slick, for they couldn't know that Mandy and Ross had already saved them. It chugged out of sight behind the rocks. Mandy let her arms drop. She sagged forward.

No; she must run to give Ross the news. She would tell him about the boat, come back up the hill and make them see her waving from Chapel Rock. Quickly Mandy slid down the slope to the place where he lay.

But she couldn't let him know how close they were to rescue. Ross was unconscious; his eyes closed, his face deathly white. Mandy leaned her head against his chest. She felt it rise and fall in shallow breaths. He was still alive. Mandy glanced down at the inlet where Selkie and Misty waited. 'Oh, make them come and help!' she pleaded. But she knew that even Selkie couldn't make sense of what she needed them to do now.

Instead, she had to do it alone. Mandy left Ross and ran for the summit once more. The patrol boat was weaving out of an inlet as she arrived. She yelled into the wind, but it snatched her voice and tossed it high on the wild currents of air. The boat turned back towards the haul-outs, searching on.

Then the sound of seals filled the air. They called high and loud from their safe harbour; a chorus of humming, singing voices. The patrol boat came back into view, as if those on board had also heard the noise.

Mandy stood with her feet wide apart, waving both arms. From the corner of her eye, she saw two seals swim out past Chapel Rock, through the narrow strait. It was Selkie and Misty going out to meet the patrol while the other seals called. The boat responded. Its engine roared; it began to speed towards her. Soon Mandy could make out Mary and Andrew in their yellow rescue-centre life-jackets, and the tall figure of her dad waving back at her. He yelled to say they'd seen her, that they were coming to fetch her.

Selkie and Misty reached the boat, circled round the back and followed it towards Chapel Rock.

'Dad, thank heavens! Ross is here too. He's injured. He's unconscious!'

'I can't hear you!' Adam Hope cupped his hands around his mouth and yelled at the top of his voice. 'Stay where you are!'

But Mandy pointed behind her. She wanted them to come round the other side of the island to get Ross off as quickly as possible.

'OK!' Adam Hope seemed to understand.

So Mandy left the summit and ran back to Ross. 'Hold on, they're coming!' She took hold of him and tried to raise his hand. His eyelids flickered, but he lay without moving.

The sound of the speeding motor drew near, then slowed. At last the Sparrowhawk appeared, gliding between the rocks. Andrew picked his way expertly towards them.

'It's Ross. Please help him,' Mandy cried, sobbing with relief.

Mary leaned over the side of the boat, across the narrow but deep channel that separated the boat from the rock. 'How badly injured is he?' Her face was as pale as Ross's, her voice desperate.

Mandy called back. 'I think he's broken his leg. He's unconscious!'

'OK, Mandy.' Adam Hope joined Mary, while Andrew Williamson held the boat on the spot. The engine chugged out exhaust fumes, and the Sparrowhawk bobbed and swayed about ten metres away from the rocks. 'Listen, you have to hold on a bit longer,' he told her.

Mandy shook her head. 'I don't think Ross can!' He lay still and pale as she cradled his head.

'You have to, both of you!'

'Get us off here, please!'

'We can't. You know that no one can come on to Castle Rock by boat. There's nowhere for us to land!'

'Please, Dad!'

'Listen, Mandy. This is as close as we can get. We'll throw blankets across for you to catch, OK?' The Sparrowhawk dipped dangerously

close to sharp rocks. Andrew had to roar the
engine into rapid reverse.

She understood. Gently she laid Ross flat on
the ground and ran to the water's edge. She
saw the boat approach again, and Adam and
Mary get ready with rolled blankets.

'OK?'

She nodded.

'Do your best!' Adam Hope leaned back and
threw her the first bundle.

Mandy stretched up and caught it. She did
the same with the second bundle from Mary.
Without waiting to be told what to do, she took

the bundles back up the slope, unrolled them and wrapped them around Ross. Inside one she found a flask filled with hot drink. She unscrewed the top and trickled some of the liquid into Ross's mouth.

'OK?' Adam Hope's anxious voice called.

'Better!' She saw Ross's eyelids flicker again. He turned his head towards the drink.

'Now listen!' Her dad's voice stayed urgent. 'We came out looking for seals after Gordon telephoned us. Your mum stayed at the rescue centre. Have you seen them?'

Mandy looked up and nodded. 'The seals are OK!' She pointed beyond the boat to the group swimming by the shore. 'We got them off the haul-outs before the oil slick hit it!'

'Brilliant! Good girl!' He gave her a thumbs-up signal. 'But now we've got another problem. Somehow we've got to get you and Ross safely off there.' He wanted her to understand that the danger wasn't over yet. 'We radioed your mum as soon as we spotted you, so she knows you're OK!'

Mandy took a deep breath. She didn't feel worried about herself. It was Ross who needed help.

Mary's voice interrupted. 'Emily knows what the problem is. She says she'll work out a way of getting you off.'

Mandy listened and nodded. Ross had opened his eyes. The blankets and the warm drink had brought him round.

'Keep calm and just stay where you are!' Adam Hope shouted. 'Between us we'll think of something!'

'What about the seals?' Ross asked for the fifth or sixth time. He could sit propped against a rock, huddled in the blankets. His broken leg stuck straight out in front of him.

'They're fine, look!' Mandy pointed towards Selkie and Misty. They swam quietly at a safe distance from the motor-boat. 'And the others aren't far away. I can see Shadow and Harmony from here. They're all safe, honestly!' It was fifteen minutes since help had first arrived; time for Ross to come round properly with the help of the blankets and the sweet drink.

'We got through to your mum again on the radiophone!' Adam Hope shouted from the boat. 'She's been in touch with the coastguard.

They're picking her up in the helicopter right now and bringing her straight over. I told you it wouldn't be long!'

'Did you hear that?' Mandy asked Ross.

He nodded. The pain in his leg made it hard for him to talk.

Soon the odd noise of a helicopter's spinning blades cut through the air. It was out of sight, but the sound was unmistakeable; a kind of whirring clatter of blades and engine. All heads turned towards the shore. The grown-ups in the boat craned their necks to see. Mandy told Ross to look up. Even the seals turned in the water to watch it appear.

The helicopter rose over Castle Hill like a heavy, clumsy bird. It swung down to the shore and kept on coming across the sea. The little seal colony swam closer to the coastline, wary of the strange sight. Only Selkie and Misty stayed close by Chapel Rock, faithful to Ross and Mandy to the end.

'Where's it going to land?' Mandy looked round at the rocky slope. There was no flat surface for the helicopter to settle on. It hovered overhead, the loud drone of its engine drowning out the chug of the patrol boat.

'It won't!' Ross stared up at the grey belly of the helicopter. 'They'll send someone down to winch us up.'

'On a rope?' Mandy didn't see how this would work for someone who was badly injured. She glanced across at her dad, but all other eyes were still fixed on the helicopter.

'Don't worry, they'll have a sling to sit in, and a harness.' Ross explained what he could remember about his dad's job as a rescue pilot. 'Look, here it comes!'

Mandy saw a door slide open in the side of the helicopter. A rope was being lowered. She caught a glimpse of the pilot in his white helmet, busy at the controls. She could see her mum leaning out of the door, looking anxiously down, and another man in a helmet getting strapped into a harness to follow the first rope down.

Slowly, inch by inch, the coastguard descended on his rope. At last he dropped gently on to the rock. He unhitched himself and bent over Ross to check his injuries. Then he got to work splinting the broken leg and folding his arm inside a strong sling. 'Only the leg looks broken,' he told them. 'The arm is probably just sprained.'

'He's been unconscious.' Mandy wanted him to know how bad it had been.

The man nodded then turned to his patient. 'You're Ross McLeod, aren't you? I'm Iain Johnstone. I used to fly with your father.' He patted Ross on the shoulder. 'You look a lot like him, as a matter of fact.' Quickly he caught hold of the other rope and began to buckle Ross inside the harness.

'You knew my dad?' Ross winced at the pain of being moved.

'Sure. He was my partner for a couple of years. A great pilot, Robert McLeod. One of the best.' He strapped Ross in securely, checking the splint on his leg.

'Were you there when he had his accident?' Ross made a grab for the coastguard's harness. The helicopter was ready to winch him clear of the rock, but he wanted an answer.

Iain nodded. 'I quit working for the oil company straight after, took this job as a coastguard instead.'

Ross listened hard.

'Your dad and I used to talk a lot about joining the coastguards. He always said he fancied this job.' Again he patted Ross's arm.

'I'll tell you one thing, son. Your dad would have been proud of you today!'

He didn't need to say any more. Ross's eyes filled with tears. Then they winched him off Chapel Rock, through the air to the safety of the helicopter.

It wasn't long before Mandy joined them. She took her last look down at the rock. There was only time to wave a quick goodbye to Selkie and watch her swim to join the rest of the seals before her mum had her in her arms. She hugged Mandy until she'd almost squeezed the breath out of her.

'I thought I said "no heroics"?' Emily Hope said when she found her voice at last.

'We're sorry, Mum.'

'Well, I should have known better than to think that you would sit by and watch a disaster happen. That wouldn't be the least bit like you, Mandy Hope!'

Then the helicopter's engine roared, and they were on their way to hospital on the mainland. They crossed the sea with its scattered islands, flew over mountains in the evening light. Mandy had a birds'-eye view of the coast, the tiny, scattered houses, the fields and at last the town where the helicopter was to land.

Paramedics ran to meet them on the landing-pad. They transferred Ross from helicopter to wheeled stretcher, and raced across the tarmac to the wide glass doors of the hospital entrance. Mandy followed on foot, holding on to her mum's arm.

'He'll be OK,' Emily Hope assured her. 'They'll take good care of him.'

Ross went straight into X-ray, and then to have his broken leg fixed. By the time Mary and Adam Hope arrived, the bone had been set, and Ross's wounds stitched. Mandy and her mother sat through it all, recovering from the near tragedy in the peace and quiet of a hospital side-ward.

'Mandy has to stay in overnight,' Mrs Hope explained. They had all gone to sit round Ross's bed; his mum, Mandy's mum and dad, and Mandy. 'They want to check her over.'

'I'm OK!' she insisted. She had nothing worse than a few cuts and bruises.

'And you'll have to stay in for forty-eight hours,' Mary warned Ross. 'Because of the concussion. They need to keep an eye on you.'

He grumbled and complained, especially when he heard that Mandy had been offered a special lift home to Kilmarten in the coast-guards' helicopter.

'There'll be other times,' Mary told him. 'Iain says you can go up with them as soon as you're better.'

Ross said nothing, but he looked pleased.

'And he says they've decided to clean up the seals' haul-outs by hand. No need to use chemicals,' Ross's mum went on. 'That should cut down the damage to wildlife and let your precious seals go back home as soon as possible.'

Mandy grinned at him. 'Aren't you sorry you'll miss that?' She planned to be part of the group of volunteers who cleaned up the oil before she had to leave Jura at the end of her holiday.

'Yes, and aren't you sorry you won't be here to see Selkie and Misty's pups when they have them?' He grinned back.

She glanced at her mum and dad. 'Who says I won't?' There was always next summer. 'I could be one of those dreadful tourists who keep on coming back . . . !'

*   *   *

And next day, as the helicopter picked her up and took her back to Jura, and she looked down once more on Selkie Bay, Mandy knew she would return.

The sun was shining on Chapel Rock as they circled over it. Iain wanted to show her that the seals had made temporary haul-outs on the rocks below the cross.

'Safe and sound,' he said, pointing to the lazy grey bodies sunning themselves below.

The seals were stretched out, yawning and curling their tails in the air. She recognised Shadow and Iona, who sat facing the shore. They seemed to be calling across the water to Castle Hill. Mandy waved goodbye.

Then the helicopter swept on towards the shore. It hovered and dropped slowly on to the beach. Iain slid the door open to let Mandy out. She jumped, ducked, then made a run away from the whirling blades. Once more she waved.

The helicopter rose and swung out across the bay. Mandy sighed. It had been a perfect ride home.

Then, as she turned to talk up Castle Hill to meet her mum and dad at the lodge, she saw

Selkie on the shore. The seal was waiting beside Gordon's salvaged boat. As Mandy went running towards her, Selkie launched herself over the pebbles, hurrying across the beach, barking her loud greeting.

Mandy flung herself to the ground and hugged the seal pup. She saw Misty waiting quietly in the shallow water. 'Thank you,' she whispered to them both. Then she let Selkie go. For Mandy this had been a wonderful holiday. She'd found friends she would remember all her life.

She watched as the seal pup tossed her head

and flopped away, heaving herself towards the waves. Selkie slipped into the shallows, immediately sleek and streamlined. When she swam to join Misty, she turned.

Mandy waved and smiled. In reply, the seal leaped almost clear of the water, plunged and disappeared once more beneath the sparkling waves.

The Animal Ark Newsletter

Would you like to receive The Animal Ark Newsletter? It has lots of news about Lucy Daniels and the Animal Ark series, plus quizzes, puzzles and competitions. It is published three times a year and is free for children who live in the United Kingdom and Ireland.

If you would like to receive it for a year,
please write to:
The Animal Ark Newsletter,
c/o Hodder Children's Books,
338 Euston Road, London NW1 3BH,
sending your name and address
(UK and Ireland only).